Under a Raging Moon

by Frank Zafiro

Wolfmont

For every officer who ever had the courage to wear a badge... and honor it.

UNDER A RAGING MOON

First printing – June 2006
Wolfmont Publishing,
Copyright ©2006 Frank Zafiro
All Rights Reserved

ISBN 0-9778-4021-2

For information, contact:
info@wolfmont.com
or
Wolfmont Publishing
PO Box 205
Ranger, GA 30734

"People sleep peaceably in their beds at night only because rough men stand ready to do violence on their behalf."
George Orwell,
English author and satirist
(1903 - 1950)

Prologue
Fall 1994

"So what do you want from me, doc?"

"I want you to tell me how you feel about what happened."

The police officer snorted. "It doesn't really matter what I say."

The doctor leaned back in his chair before answering. He studied the man across from him. The officer sat in a relaxed position, his feet crossed at the ankles. Both hands lay across his lap. The doctor saw the bandaged arm and shoulder and a leg brace, as well as the cane leaning next to the officer, all evidence of the injuries he had sustained. He noticed none of the defensive body language he usually encountered in interviews such as this one. The officer appeared physically fit, his muscles well-formed even in a relaxed state. He met the doctor's gaze with a frank, even stare. No challenge resided in his eyes, but none of his inner thoughts were betrayed, either.

"Officer, please understand. I do not work directly for the Department. I am contracted to do an evaluation after a critical incident and render a professional opinion. You are required—"

"Required to cooperate fully as a condition of employment. Failure to do so may result in suspension or termination." The officer smiled without humor.

The doctor tried a different tactic. "It may help you

to talk about it."

The officer shrugged but said nothing.

The doctor suppressed a sigh, leaned back in his chair, and opened the officer's personnel file. He had already reviewed it, of course. He always made a point to know as much as possible about his patients before he sat down with them. Nothing in the file indicated the man was any different from any other cop he'd interviewed. Still, he found police officers to be a pleasant distraction from his regular practice of rich and whiny men and women. Some cops were uncultured ex-jocks, but many had a combination of intelligence and culture blended with a blue-collar worker's outlook that fascinated him. The effect of power on the individual also made these interviews well worth his time. He only charged the City forty percent of what he charged his civilian clientele. It only seemed fair, since these interviews were fueling a paper he was writing for a psychiatric journal.

"What do they say about me in there?" The officer asked, nodding toward the personnel file.

"Lots of things," the doctor replied, unsure if he had detected sarcasm in the officer's voice or not. "It says you graduated third in your class at the academy. You have been a police officer for just three years and during that time you've had no sustained internal affairs investigations. There have been seven unsustained complaints, however. Other than that, your last performance review was very complimentary."

"Company man," the officer said. This time the sarcasm in his voice was unmistakable.

The doctor looked up again and caught the officer's eye. He saw a flicker of emotion. It disappeared quickly and he wondered if he had seen it at all.

"I am required to fill out a general report regarding your mental and emotional fitness for duty. A satisfactory response is as important as your physical recovery with regards to your return to full duty."

At the words 'full duty,' the officer winced slightly.

The doctor pressed on. "However, everything you say within the confines of this office is entirely confidential. By law, I cannot reveal it to anyone, nor can I be compelled to by any court." The doctor watched as the officer processed the information.

The officer, silent for several moments, finally said, "Doc...you wanna know the truth?"

The doctor nodded.

"The truth is...it felt good. I did what I had to do and I don't feel bad for that." He chewed his lip a moment, then continued. "That's the problem. I feel bad because I don't feel bad about that. I feel good about it. I'd do it again."

The doctor nodded slowly. Now the session had truly begun.

Monday, August 12th, 1994
Graveyard Shift

Crack!

The flashlight hit the pavement. Thomas Chisolm looked up from his note pad to see his rookie, Maurice Payne, looking sheepish. Payne grabbed the light and checked it. Relief flooded his face when it still worked.

Chisolm struggled not to shake his head in disgust. Payne had already spent three times longer than he should have putting the police car through its pre-flight check. To make matters worse, he'd managed to forget half the procedures.

How in the hell did this kid made it through his first two Field Training Officers? Chisolm wondered. *Christ, how did he make it through the Police Academy?*

Payne finally settled into the seat and started the engine. He carefully turned on and off every emergency light, including the yelp and wail sirens. Satisfied, he started to put the car into gear.

"Forget something?" Chisolm asked in as neutral a voice as he could muster.

Payne looked worried and confused.

Jesus, this kid flusters easy, Chisolm thought. He'd acted the same way earlier when Chisolm pointed out that he forgot to check the back seat.

Payne's worried look grew almost frantic. He

4

looked to Chisolm for the answer. The veteran put his hand on the shotgun, which sat right beside the radio, its barrel pointing upward.

"Oh." Payne put the car in park and released the shotgun.

"Do it outside," Chisolm instructed in a gentle voice. *For the fifteenth time*, he groused inwardly.

Payne unloaded the shotgun, cleared it and reloaded it. In his attempt to do it faster than his abilities allowed, it took him nearly twice as long.

"Easy, son," Chisolm told him. "Take your time and do it right."

Payne finished clumsily and replaced the shotgun in its rack. He picked up the radio and checked them into service. Chisolm winced at the rookie's voice. It sounded weak and mush-mouth, carrying no authority at all.

Reflecting briefly, Chisolm knew why Payne had made it through two Field Training Officers. He had been on a couple of calls where compassion had been the order of the day and he had to admit the kid did a superb job. A rape victim is not an easy person to communicate with, especially for a male officer. Some victims demanded a female officer for that very reason, but Payne had been able to establish an excellent rapport with the victim, kept her emotions in check and took a good report.

Still, there was more to the job than being compassionate. Chisolm had long ago learned to save his compassion for those who deserved it. A cop had to be strong enough to be gentle, but he had to remain strong.

Chisolm recalled the incident right before the weekend, when a gang member had come close to assaulting Payne. Chisolm had seen it coming, but let Payne go with it as far as he safely could. The nice-guy routine doesn't always work, especially when a street-wise gang banger is yelling, "Kiss my black ass, you white pig!"

A cop had to wear many hats, Chisolm knew: counselor, confessor, friend, philosopher, detective, hard-ass, just to name a few. Those who failed to understand this were weak officers, even if they excelled in one area. Like Payne. Or like Kahn, who was a hard-ass all the time and got complaints by the trunk load.

The night passed slowly, giving Chisolm plenty of time for reflection. Payne took way too long to accomplish even the simplest of tasks. A traffic stop became a major ordeal for him, which Chisolm considered ridiculous this far into his training. His officer safety bordered on critically poor, something Chisolm found unforgivable. Not only did that endanger Payne, but anyone who worked around him.

Chisolm let out a sigh as he stood safely behind the curtain of light at the front tire of the patrol car. Payne patiently explained to the woman in the mini-van what constituted running a red light. "Jesus, lady," Chisolm muttered to himself, "if you knew how long and hard he worked on that, you'd just sign it."

Payne eventually got her signature and concluded

the stop. Once back in the car, he reached for the radio to clear when a shrill alert tone sounded.

"Dispatch to all units. Receiving an armed robbery alarm at 1527 N. Birch, 7-11 store." The dispatcher's voice intoned. *"Hold-up alarm, 1527 N. Birch."*

"Go!" shouted Chisolm and grabbed the mike. He listened in frustration as several units attempted to answer at once, covering each other with a harsh buzz.

"Coverage," stated the operator. *"Receiving further. Suspect is a single, white male wearing black jeans, white shirt with long dark hair. Also has a scar down the left side of his face. Suspect displayed a black revolver. Fled westbound on foot."*

"C'mon!" Chisolm yelled. Same damn guy, the one everyone called Scarface.

Payne approached the red light at Indiana and Post. His hand hovered over the emergency light controls as if he couldn't decide whether to use lights or both lights and siren.

"Just drive," Chisolm told him, punching the lights. At two-thirty in the morning on a Monday night, not much traffic to worry about.

"Adam-116, I'm a couple off. I'll check westbound."

Chisolm recognized Katie MacLeod's steady voice.

"Baker-123, in the area to the south. Also."
Chisolm recognized Stefan Kopriva's solid voice.
Another good troop.

"Go ahead, Baker-123."

"Do we have a K-9 working?"

A pause. Then, *"Negative. Do you want us to call
one out?"*

"Affirm."

Good call, Chisolm thought. *Maybe we'll catch the
guy this time.*

Payne drove right past the turn on Monroe Street.
He realized it half a block later and started to slow.

"No," Chisolm instructed him. "Go up to Ash,
we'll back Katie."

"Adam-113, on scene at the 7-11 for the report."

Chisolm shook his head. Adam-113, Cliff Simms,
was always willing to take a report if it meant not
getting in harm's way. Otherwise, forget it.

Ash was a one-way arterial southbound, but Payne
still drove way too cautiously for Chisolm's liking.
At Maxwell, he directed him to turn right as he saw
Katie's lights.

"Baker-123, I'll be mobile on Boone west of—"

The buzz of radio transmission coverage cut him
off.

"Baker-123, copy," replied the dispatcher. *"Other unit?"*

Chisolm knew Katie was out of the car and running as soon as the transmission began.

"Adam-116... foot pursuit... south bound from my car's location. We're going through... construction yard..."

Chisolm got on the air before the dispatcher could respond. "Adam-112, her vehicle is parked at Maxwell and Cannon. We'll swing around and come in from the southwest."

"Copy."

"Baker-123, coming in from the southeast."

"Copy."

"Take Belt," Chisolm ordered sharply. He didn't care about training at this point. Katie was running around in the dark with an armed robber. She needed backup.

"This is L-123. All other units set-up a perimeter, four blocks in each direction," Sgt. Miyamoto Shen said, his voice calm and authoritative.

No one answered, leaving the radio clear for Adam-116.

At the corner of Belt and Sinto, Chisolm directed Payne to turn left. The rookie did so, still way too slow for his liking.

"Hit all your lights. Everything. Light up that

yard." He pointed at the construction yard to the northeast. An eight-foot fence ran all along the south side of the yard. *Good*, thought Chisolm, already out of the car and scanning for movement. *That should slow him down.*

Payne clambered out of the car, knocking his side-handle baton out of its holder. It clattered onto the pavement. Chisolm ignored him, continuing to scan from behind the curtain of light created by the patrol vehicle's spotlight, high beams and takedown light located on the roof in the light bar.

Nothing. Fifteen seconds of nothing on the air from Katie. Then twenty. Radio should check on—

"Adam-116, an update," came the dispatcher's voice.

There was a terrible moment of silence. Chisolm's gun was drawn and at the low-ready position. He saw Payne in his peripheral vision and watched the rookie mimic his stance.

"I got him, he's running near the south fence." Katie's voice was labored and tense. *"Westbound."*

"Copy. Westbound near the south fence. Baker-123?"

"I'm almost there," Stefan Kopriva replied.

Then where the hell were they? Chisolm thought.

There!

He saw a figure, short and slender, running hard

near the fence. The figure pulled up short, probably noticing the lights. Chisolm drew a bead on the figure, trying to see his hands but unable to at this distance.

"Adam-112, I see him about mid-block," Chisolm told radio.

There was a flash of light from the figure's hand and a loud bang.

"Shots fired!" called Katie.

Chisolm carefully aimed at the figure, but held his fire. The danger of cross-fire was too great. He would give Katie and Stef a few seconds to take cover, at least.

The suspect climbed the fence. He went over it military style with almost no effort, climbed rapidly up one side, swung over the top and then dropped to the ground in two quick, controlled movements. He landed in a crouch and immediately fired in Chisolm's direction. Chisolm heard the sound of shattering glass as he returned fire, squeezing off three quick rounds. The muzzle flash took away his already minimal night vision. He scanned for movement but saw none.

"Adam-112 to -14, do you see him?" Chisolm keyed the mike with his left hand while keeping his pistol pointed where he'd last seen the suspect.

"We've taken cover here in the yard. We lost visual on him as soon as he fired."

"Copy. -12 to radio, he may have fled southbound."

"Copy, southbound."

Chisolm heard a moan from the driver's side and glanced over. Payne was gone. The spotlight was dark. Chisolm ran around the back end of the car and saw Payne collapsed on the ground holding his face. He could see dark blood next to him and seeping through his hands.

"Adam-112, officer down," Chisolm spoke into his portable radio. "I need medics to my location."

Radio copied his transmission as he knelt next to Payne, still keeping his weapon trained on the threat area. "Payne?" He asked gently.

Payne moaned. "It hurts."

Chisolm pulled Payne's hand away from his cheek and saw the cut. It was two inches long and had probably been caused by flying glass after the spotlight had been hit.

"You'll be okay," he said through gritted teeth, then keyed the mike. "Adam-112, injuries are a facial laceration, not life-threatening."

"Copy, I'll inform medics."

Chisolm stood by with Payne as a dog handler arrived on scene and began a track. He remained alert but at Payne's side for twenty minutes during the track until it was called off. The K-9 officer advised that it was likely that the suspect had gotten into a vehicle at Sharp and Elm.

Medics, who had been standing off until the area was declared secure, arrived and treated Payne, who seemed to be slipping into shock. Chisolm watched as they wiped the cut with iodine and put a gauze pad against it to stem the bleeding, which had slowed to a trickle. An ambulance transported Payne to Sacred Heart Hospital.

As the ambulance pulled away, Chisolm picked up Payne's gun and put it in his briefcase. The young officer had not asked about it once. Chisolm felt sorry for him. Not only because he'd been hurt but also because it was very apparent that he was shortly going to have to recommend that Payne be fired.

What the hell, Chisolm thought. *I was his teacher, his doctor and now I am going to be the axe-man. Bad night for us all.*

Thomas Chisolm, despite being a fourteen-year veteran of the police department and former Green Beret with two tours in Vietnam, could not shake the sinking feeling in his chest as he kicked the shards of glass from the spotlight to the curb of the street. He couldn't stop wondering how much worse it was going to get.

Tuesday, August 13th
Day Shift

Karl Winter made his way into the roll call room for his fifth day shift of the week. He walked past the sergeants' offices and the lieutenant's office to get there, but didn't even turn his head. Despite their rank, he held most of his superiors in contempt. Besides, he remembered when all of them were rookies who could hardly keep from handcuffing themselves instead of the suspect.

Officer Stefan Kopriva passed him on the way out of the locker room. The graveyard officer had changed into plain clothes before heading home.

"Get some sleep, kid," Winter said.

"G'night," Kopriva said, his voice a tired croak as he headed down the hallway.

Winter remembered those days well enough. Kopriva had three or four years on the job, and he'd spend quite a few more on graveyard before he gained enough seniority to bid another shift.

Not me, Winter thought, and smiled inwardly. Nine months to go and he'd retire. Not long. Just like waiting for a baby to be born. Only the delivery would be a piece of cake and when it was over, he and Mary would sell the house and move up to the lake cabin where he planned to catch so many fish they'd have to re-stock the lake.

Winter's thick mouth broke into a half-smile at the thought.

The roll call room was unimpressive and square, with three large tables, one for each sector. Most of the shift was already present. Winter walked toward his seat at the Charlie sector table. He noticed several graveyard patrol officers at the back of the room, working on reports.

"Milking the system, Chisolm?" Winter asked.

Chisolm looked up. The intense look on his face melted and he grinned at Winter. "Call me a dairy maid."

Winter chuckled. "Nine months, Tommy."

"Nine months and you drop that baby elephant you're carrying?" Chisolm grinned.

Winter ran his hand over his uniform shirt, which was stretched tightly over his large stomach. "Ah, screw you. Nine months and I retire."

"Oh, hell, Karl. You've been retired on the job for years now."

"I say again, screw you. You're just jealous." Karl gloated. "What do you have left? Six, seven years?"

"*You're* jealous."

"Me? Why? Because I don't get to work graveyard and live like a vampire?"

"No," Chisolm said evenly, "You're jealous because I get to eat your wife but not her cooking."

Karl exhaled heavily into the silence. No way he

could top that one without sounding lame. Chisolm's eyes danced mischievously as he waited.

Finally Winter said, "Oh, go back to shafting the taxpayers out of their tax dollars, you O-T whore."

Chisolm chuckled and returned to his report.

Insults and jokes flew across the room, while others discussed everything but police work. Cars, boats, sports and hunting were popular topics. The two rookies assigned to the shift sat rigidly in their chairs, speaking only when spoken to, obviously uncomfortable in the midst of so much seniority.

Will Reiser tossed a travel brochure to Winter. It featured Cancún, Mexico, and a smiling blonde in a bathing suit walking along a sandy white beach next to a light blue ocean.

"Whattya think, Karl?" he asked. "Good enough for a twenty-year anniversary?"

Winter thumbed through it briefly, nodding. It was a good idea. Police wives go through a lot in a twenty-year career. Will's wife Patty deserved a trip like this. So did his Mary, for that matter.

"You bet. Good choice." He slid the brochure back to him. Rookies coming on now had a new retirement system and had to do thirty years or until age fifty-five. He felt sorry for their wives.

Sergeant David Poole entered the room and sat wordlessly at the head of Winter's table. He looked grouchier than usual. Winter didn't find that surprising. Poole had made sergeant before Alan

Hart, who was now a lieutenant. Poole had helped Hart study and brought him along. Once Hart made sergeant, the two were bosom buddies. After Hart made lieutenant, he suddenly became too good for a lowly three-striper and began dumping on Poole. Worse yet, Poole had become an effective, if reluctant, suck-up.

Lieutenant Alan Hart entered the room and talk quickly subsided. Winter knew Hart thought it was out of respect for him, but in reality, no one wanted him to over-hear anything. In a profession of strong-willed men and women, Winter saw an awful lot of disagreement but there was one thing universally agreed upon: everyone loathed Lt. Hart. Even the boot-lickers who sucked up to him didn't like him.

Hart was either unaware of this fact or didn't care. He stepped up to the lectern and looked around the room slowly before calling everyone to order. "Listen up. Several stolens last night."

Only the two rookies wrote in their notebooks as the lieutenant read off four license plates belonging to stolen vehicles.

Hart continued, "Anybody seen Gregory Macdonald? Black male, hangs out down on the Block? Detective Browning wants to talk to him. Call him anytime day or night."

He shuffled papers, skipping an irrelevant memo, then said, "Captain Reott is looking for volunteers for the Cops-2-Kids program. Two from each shift. Paid as overtime. Any volunteers?"

Anthony Giovanni spoke up, "Lieutenant, no one

wants to do that because Channel Two puts you on T.V."

Hart's eyes narrowed. "I have one volunteer. Thank you, Tony. Any others?"

No one even breathed.

"Okay, well, there will be a volunteer by roll call tomorrow or I will designate one. And Tony," he turned to face the officer, "since Channel Two is paying for everything but your time on this project, don't you think they deserve a little of the publicity?"

Giovanni didn't respond. Winter knew what the officer thought and figured he and everyone else in the room knew how difficult it was for Gio not to say it.

Hart held his stare for a moment, then moved the memo to the back of the stack.

"Okay. Graveyard had another armed robbery tonight in Adam Sector. The 7-11 at Birch and Maxwell was hit. Suspect fled westbound. Officer MacLeod gave chase through the lumber yard at Maxwell and Elm..." Hart looked up and directed his gaze toward the back of the room. "Officer MacLeod?"

Winter turned to look at Katie, who looked up from her report. "Sir?"

"The suspect was armed?" Hart asked.

"Yes, sir. He displayed a black revolver."

"Same description as the other Scarface robberies?"

MacLeod nodded.

"And you chased this man through a construction yard in the dark?"

MacLeod nodded again.

Hart looked around the room of assembled officers. "Let's learn from this, people. Is it safe to pursue an armed robber alone into a dark construction yard? Or would it be better to set up a perimeter and wait for back up?"

"She had back up." Chisolm stared coldly at Lt. Hart. The thin white scar that ran from Chisolm's temple to his chin pulsed with hatred.

"Sir," MacLeod said calmly, "perhaps this is something you would like to discuss with my lieutenant?"

Hart blanched as if just struck with a one-two punch. The tension in the room had jumped noticeably and a couple of day-shifters chuckled surreptitiously at Hart's dilemma.

Typical, Winter thought. Hart wasn't diddly on the street and now he is the ultimate Monday-morning quarterback. It was no wonder Scarface hadn't been caught yet, with people like Hart directing the response. Winter admired MacLeod for standing up to him. The girl had grit.

Hart recovered quickly, brushing aside the exchange. "I understand the suspect fired several shots at officers. A trainee was wounded. Yours, I think, Tom?"

A rumble erupted from the tables. Winter shook his head in disbelief. Officers were involved in a shooting last night and Hart leads off the briefing with stolen vehicles and some community program?

Chisolm appeared to ignore the grumbling and locked his glare onto Hart. "It will be in my report, Lieutenant." He then lowered his eyes to the paper in front of him and resumed writing.

Winter smiled, glad his back was to Hart. Another bureaucrat trying to screw with Tom Chisolm. *Good luck, Al. You haven't been successful yet.*

Hart moved on. "This is the eleventh robbery in two weeks. The department is starting to look like the Keystone Cop Brigade. Double…no, *triple* your checks of all convenience stores and fast food restaurants. Everyone understand? And you might want to think about canceling breakfast until this guy is caught. It looks bad to see four police cars at a restaurant with Scarface out robbing places."

Screw you, Hart, Winter thought, knowing everyone in the room shared his sentiment.

"Anyone have anything for the shift?"

No reply.

"Okay, then, hit the streets." There was a scraping of chairs as everyone stood and gathered their gear. Hart shifted his gaze to Chisolm. "Officer Chisolm, I'll need to see you in my office."

Chisolm nodded. "As soon as my report is complete."

"No, now."

"Lieutenant, the Captain wants a copy of this report on his desk right away, since there was an injury and shots fired." Chisolm spoke in an even voice.

"Fine," Hart's tone was curt. "As *soon* as you finish."

"Yes, sir," Chisolm answered, his respect a hollow echo.

Hart gathered his papers and left the room.

What a prick, Winter thought. From the look on his face, Thomas Chisolm was thinking the exact same thing.

***

Breakfast was holy writ for the day tour. Everyone knew it, including the radio dispatchers. Day shift dispatchers routinely held low-priority report calls to allow the officers their break. The oft-given justification was that once things got busy, there was a strong chance that the officer would not get a lunch later on. This was rarely true.

Eliza's Café was seven blocks from the station and a favorite of the south-side day tour. Winter arrived to find Will Reiser and Mark Ridgeway already half a cup down.

"Can you believe that prick Hart?" Reiser asked

Winter as he sat down.

"Been that way since he got the gold bar," Winter responded, waving at Eliza and mouthing the word coffee.

Ridgeway, a seventeen-year veteran who was one of the fittest men on the department, sat glumly at the table. "Hart," he said in a bitter voice, "is so stupid he couldn't find his ass with both hands and a flashlight."

Eliza brought Winter's coffee. "What are we chuckling about today, my evil little policeman?"

For a woman who looked like everyone's grandmother, Winter was often surprised at what came out of her mouth.

"We were discussing the virtues of our superior officers," Reiser told her with a wink.

"Oh, you mean what a horse's patoot Lt. Alan Hart has become." Eliza returned the wink before turning to Winter. "The usual, Karl?"

Karl considered the offer, then declined. "Just coffee this morning, sweetie."

Eliza shrugged. "Is anyone going to eat this morning?"

"Gio will," Reiser said. "Hart volunteered him for something at roll call. You can probably start the French toast now."

Eliza walked away, saying, "If he doesn't show, I'm charging you for it, William Reiser the Third."

Reiser grinned.

The three men talked easily for several minutes, though Winter and Reiser carried the conversation. Ridgeway muttered an occasional response, then returned to sipping his coffee.

Ten minutes later, Anthony Giovanni entered and slumped into his seat. He looked at each of the three men in turn, then asked, "Is that Hart a raging prick or what?"

All three men nodded sympathetically.

Giovanni continued. "Try to tell the guy why there are no volunteers and I get hammered. I should call my Guild rep and file a grievance."

"Why don't you?"

Giovanni shrugged. "It *is* overtime."

"Charlie-257 and a unit to back," squawked the portable radios of all four men.

Giovanni cursed. "I just checked out here." Then to radio, "-257, go ahead."

"An alarm, 5103 E. Trent, KayPlus parts. No zoning."

Giovanni copied the call and looked at all three men. "That vindictive wench."

All three immediately understood. Thirty-two year old Giovanni was one of the youngest men on day shift. Fit, tall and dark, he made use of his physical assets when it came to dating. A self-proclaimed womanizer, Giovanni made no bones about his intentions and he made no promises. And given that, he couldn't understand what the hell was wrong with these women who all ended up hating him so much.

Irina was the third dispatcher Giovanni had dated briefly and then stopped calling. In each case, he ended up getting hammered on calls for quite some time after the breakup.

Winter chuckled. He didn't really approve of Giovanni's dating habits, but he had to admit he had lived vicariously through him on occasion. Twenty-four years of marriage, even a happy marriage, was not as outwardly exciting as Giovanni's many conquests.

"I'll take it," Reiser said, finishing his coffee and notifying radio. Ridgeway did the same. All four men could hear the slight tone of irritation as Irina copied their transmissions.

"You know," Reiser said as he left, "Janice would not let this type of thing go on. She might not have been a supervisor but she would still put that Irina in line right now." He snapped his fingers.

"Too bad she went to graveyard," Ridgeway muttered. "Abandoned us."

Eliza put a huge plate of French toast in front of Giovanni.

"My God, Eliza, I can't eat all of this," he protested.

"You'll eat it and you'll like it, Antonio Vittorio Giovanni," Eliza told him, refilling Winter's coffee.

"I won't eat all day and night after this," Giovanni muttered and dug into the pile of buttered, syrupy bread. In between bites, he complained bitterly to Winter about Irina. He didn't understand what her problem was. They went out, they had fun, they had some great sex and now he was done. He didn't want to be tied down, he wasn't looking for a relationship and he had told her that right from the beginning. Well, maybe not the very beginning, but pretty early on.

Poor Gio, thought Winter. *He really doesn't understand.*

"Gio, listen. Everyone knows your reputation. Still, a lot of women think maybe they're the one that can change you."

Giovanni snorted around a mouthful of food. "Fat chance. There ain't a woman alive."

Winter didn't answer. He hated to admit that twenty-four years ago, there was a man who felt and acted much the same way. That man had been wrong. And the woman's name had been Mary.

***

Chisolm was almost two hours into overtime when he burned off a copy of his report on the copier and put it in the Captain's box. He turned the original into Sgt. Poole, since his own sergeant had already gone home. Tired and in a bad mood, he was not particularly looking forward to seeing Hart.

Hart was in his office waiting for him. Chisolm knocked and stood by while the lieutenant continued to write something. Chisolm doubted it was anything important and figured Hart just wanted to make him wait.

After almost a minute, Hart looked up. "Come in. Close the door."

Chisolm obeyed.

A plastic chair faced the desk. Chisolm once heard that Hart had purposefully brought in a small chair that sat low to the ground to intimidate his visitors. Hart made no offer for Chisolm to be seated. Chisolm made no move toward the chair. A brief battle of wills ensued until Hart surrendered.

"Officer Chisolm," he said with exaggerated formality, "as you know, I am the Officer-in-Charge of the FTO program. I would like your appraisal of Officer Trainee Maurice Payne."

Chisolm set his briefcase on the chair. "Lieutenant, I have been quite specific in my reports."

"Nonetheless, I would like a verbal to-date report," Hart insisted.

"Fine." Chisolm crossed his arms and gave Hart a hard look. "I think that Trainee Payne should be dismissed."

"On what grounds?"

"Incompetence."

"Incompetence?" Hart raised his eyebrows. "Explain."

"It's all in my reports," Chisolm repeated.

Hart raised his voice, "I want a verbal explanation right now, Officer Chisolm. Is that clear?"

"Clear." Chisolm bit off the word.

"Now, on what grounds do you feel he should be dismissed?" Hart clearly enjoyed his power trip.

Chisolm sniffed a short breath, and then began. "Quite simply, Lieutenant, he is not cut out to be a police officer. His officer safety is almost non-existent, his knowledge of the city streets is poor and his judgment under stress is almost always wrong."

"His previous two FTOs rated him better than that," Hart pointed out.

"They were too easy on him. Besides, one of his tours was swing shift and he frequently got tied up on early calls. He can establish rapport with people and his high marks are generally in those areas." Chisolm paused. "He has weakness in every area except that one."

"Not tough enough, huh?" Hart's voice was sarcastic.

"The kid is afraid of his own shadow."

"That kid," Hart reminded him, "is going to get several stitches in his face."

Chisolm shrugged. He knew a lot of officers with scars.

Hart stood and walked around to the side of the desk and sat on the edge. "Don't you think you're being a little harsh, Tom? I mean, I had my share of difficulties early on. Hell, we all did as we came up. Why are you being so hard on this kid?"

Hart's chummy mode made Chisolm's stomach churn. *What an arrogant, condescending prick,* he thought. "Lieutenant, if you had these problems as a trainee, maybe you should have been dismissed, too."

There was a long moment of silence as Hart stared at Chisolm, disbelieving. His face turned white, then red.

"You can't talk to me like that!" he yelled, spittle flying from his lips.

Chisolm stood stock-still, his countenance unchanging.

Hart's face and hands trembled with fury. "You... you're hereby suspended from the FTO program. I want your daily log, your weekly file and your key to the file cabinet."

Chisolm showed no surprise. He opened his briefcase and withdrew all three items and dropped them with a thunk on Hart's desk.

"Payne will be re-assigned to someone who is not such a burn-out," Hart said through gritted teeth.

"He may need this, then." Chisolm slammed Payne's pistol down on Hart's desk. The slide was locked to the rear and the magazine had been removed. Chisolm tossed the magazine to Hart, catching him by surprise. Hart juggled the mag, then dropped it.

Chisolm ignored him, gathered up his briefcase and strode out the door.

***

Thwack!

Two halves of the firewood fell off the splitting block and onto an already sizable pile. Karl Winter stepped forward and tossed them aside into his stacking pile and set another round on the block. He removed the axe and stepped back.

Winter had once heard that cutting wood is a favorite activity of men. That's because it is hard work and one sees immediate results. Who said that? Mark Twain? Winter wasn't sure but he agreed with the sentiment.

He set up and swung easily, letting the weight of the axe do most of the work. Two pieces leapt apart as if in pain when the axe struck, landing several feet to each side.

Winter chopped most of his wood in the summer, storing it for the winter season. He hated chopping wood in the cold. Actually, he avoided doing anything in the cold. Besides, there was something satisfying about swinging an axe under the August sun and sweating from honest work. Police work was hard, dangerous at times, but not physically demanding, except in small bursts. His protruding belly spoke to the truth of that.

He set up another piece and continued chopping at a leisurely, constant pace. His mind whirred. This Scarface situation bothered him. The guy threatened clerks with a gun and now he was shooting at cops. Add to that the fact that the administration bungled their handling of the situation so far, both within the department and with the media. But most of all, it rankled him that the bastard was getting away with it.

Eleven stores in two weeks!

Thwack. Another piece of wood ready for burning in three months.

Winter reviewed the information he had. The description was always the same. The robber made no attempt to disguise himself. He either didn't care, or... he wanted to be seen. Which would mean he wore a disguise. Probably the hair. A good wig, maybe, giving him long hair.

What about the scar? He considered the question, but decided it was probably real. One of the clerks would have noticed a fake scar.

So the robber runs out of the store, goes three or four blocks on foot, maybe less, and gets into a car. Every track that Winter knew of ended with the K-9 officer saying the suspect probably used a car. Officers are set up on perimeter and looking for a white male with long black hair on foot. Does he slip out with his short hair and in a car?

Maybe.

Winter swung the axe lightly, sticking it into the block. He began to stack the wood.

Probably not. An officer would stop someone that even vaguely matched the description, car or not. And how close did you have to be to see the scar?

He might be able to slip out two or three times, but not eleven.

So what then?

Winter shook his head and tossed the wood into the stack. He knew the detectives in Major Crimes had more information they weren't putting out to patrol. Part of it was security and some it was the ridiculous game of ownership. They wanted to keep the information to themselves and they wanted to catch the bad guy instead of patrol. After all, why waste information on a bunch of patrolmen? They were just cops who weren't smart enough to make detective, right?

Winter frowned. He had to stop hanging out with Ridgeway. He was getting more negative by the day.

So he gets in the car and drives away... or maybe someone else is driving?

An accomplice?

Winter smiled. Of course.

A *woman*. That's how he does it.

Winter resisted the urge to hoot and holler. Hot damn, it was so easy once you saw it!

He robs the store, then runs to the car and hops in. He lays down in the back seat or something. Maybe covers up with a blanket. The woman driver gets on an arterial and drives two miles an hour under the speed limit in one direction. Five minutes later, they are way out of the area and safe.

All the cops in the city are either back near the store that he just robbed or they are running lights and siren to get there.

Not bad. I'll bet that is how he does it.

With the last piece stacked, Winter returned to the chopping block and with exuberance cut a few more pieces. He wondered if the detectives or the crime analysis unit had figured this out yet.

Then he wondered why this guy felt like he had to rob a store every day and a half. That was a hell of a lot of exposure.

Winter's brow furrowed. He set up a piece of wood and stepped back to chop it. Another small mystery.

The back door opened and Mary approached carrying a glass of iced tea. Winter admired her slender frame for a moment, but found himself drawn as usual to her face and to the laughing eyes that stared into him. Her dark hair was pulled back into a clip. He smiled when he noticed the single large strand that always pulled free and hung loosely on her cheek.

"Take a break, Grizzly Adams," she said lightly, handing him the tall glass.

Winter took it and drank deeply. Mary's tea had always been bitter, something he'd never had the heart to tell her. Eventually, he'd grown to like the taste. Inside the house, he could hear the stereo playing and recognized a Springsteen tune, *Thunder Road*. He lowered the glass and let out a satisfied sigh.

"Thanks, sweetheart."

"You're welcome." She smiled at him and Winter felt his heart melt. Forty-four years old, and she still made him feel like a schoolboy.

Winter remembered when he would play Springsteen songs for her on his acoustic guitar. His voice was horrible and his guitar playing mediocre, but he had passion. He took several rock songs and slowed them down, doing them acoustically and, he tried, romantically.

Her favorite was *Thunder Road*, partially because the woman in it was named Mary. Years later, Springsteen himself did an acoustic version of that song on M-TV. Winter broke his vow never to watch that channel and tuned in for the show. After it was over, Mary leaned against him and kissed his temple. He could still remember her warm breath in his ear as she whispered, "I liked your version better."

Winter stared at her and took another drink of the bitter tea. It was cold. Mary looked back at him with a small smile playing on her lips.

"Are you going to chop wood all day?" she asked coyly.

Winter glanced at the dying sun, then back at her. He shook his head. "No. Not all day."

Mary took the iced tea from his hand and set it on the chopping block. She gathered both his hands in hers and led him up the back steps to their house.

Karl Winter found that he had forgotten all about the Scarface robberies.

Wednesday, August 14th
Graveyard Shift

Stefan Kopriva blocked the punch and twisted to his right, snapping out a short round kick toward Shen's abdomen. The lithe sergeant dropped his elbow, catching the top of Kopriva's foot with the point.

Kopriva grunted in pain, but pulled the foot back and fired it at Shen's head.

Shen leaned away from the kick, then slid underneath and swept Kopriva's supporting leg out from under him.

Kopriva fell hard to the mat, his breath whooshing out.

Shen remained merciless, dropping next to him and reaching in for a choke-hold.

Kopriva rolled out of range and stood up without using his hands. Shen pounced upon him almost instantly, flicking a punch toward his face. Kopriva blocked it with his left and countered with a straight right to Shen's rib-cage. It landed with a solid thud. Shen exhaled with a grunt and stepped back.

"Time!" yelled Chisolm.

Kopriva and Shen bowed to each other and shook hands, both breathing heavily.

"Nice work, Stef."

Kopriva shook his head. "Nice work? Nah, that foot sweep you made was excellent. *That* was nice work."

Shen rubbed his ribs. "That last punch will stick with me for a bit."

They thanked Chisolm for timing the round. The veteran officer winked at Kopriva. "Any chance to see someone beat on a sergeant, I'm there," he said, and returned to the weight bench and resumed lifting.

Shen laughed. "I'm sure that's a common sentiment."

"Depends on the sergeant," Chisolm said his voice straining as he curled the hand weights, "but I can't discriminate." He grimaced with effort, trying to affect a smile.

Kopriva walked with Shen from the gym down the hall to the locker room. He knew that some of the other graveyard patrolmen called him "Sergeant's Boy" because he sparred with Shen a few times a week. He didn't care. They called him a "Code-Four Cowboy," too, because he didn't like calling for back-up.

Sticks and stones.

At his locker, he undressed and headed for the shower. The hot water felt good as it cascaded down his body. When he returned to his locker and began dressing, he read through the small phrases of positive self-talk taped to the inside of his locker door. They served to get him into the right mind-set for patrol every night.

I will survive, no matter what, even if I am hit, read the final one.

Below that, he had written *I am a warrior, in mind, body and spirit.*

Kopriva slipped his bullet-proof vest over his head and secured the straps into place. *A warrior's armor.*

Below the positive self-talk, he'd hung a narrow bamboo wall-hanging. Painted upon the horizontal bamboo slats was a Japanese style tiger and a yellowing moon, tendrils of smoke or clouds snaking across it. It had been a gift from his *sensei* when he achieved his black belt two years ago. He called it "Tiger Under A Raging Moon" and said that the brooding cat reminded him of Kopriva.

Now, two years later, Kopriva still wasn't quite sure why.

He strapped his duty belt into place and removed his .40-caliber Glock pistol from the holster. A quick check showed a full magazine and one in the pipe. He slid the gun back into the holster, closed his locker and made his way to roll call.

***

"Listen up," Lieutenant Robert Saylor said as he stepped to the lectern at the front of the room.

The drill hall fell silent.

Saylor read through a couple of administrative memos, then paused and looked out at the assembled group of police officers.

"Last night," he began, "we had officers fired upon by the Scarface robber. One of them was injured when a bullet struck a spotlight. That's going to be a charge of attempted murder, or at least first degree assault, when Scarface is apprehended. And it is one more very good reason to catch this son of a bitch."

General agreement murmured through the room.

"El-tee?" Chisolm said.

Saylor nodded for him to continue.

"I believe this guy might have a military background," Chisolm said. "He went over that fence military style. Besides that, he fired a shot our direction almost as soon as he landed."

Saylor considered. "Did you get that information to Rene in Crime Analysis?"

Chisolm nodded. "I sent a copy of my report along with a note."

"Good work." Saylor turned his attention to the rest of the patrol officers. "That information should heighten your caution, ladies and gentlemen. This guy may not be some doped up mope who doesn't know which end of the barrel is the working end. He may know your tactics and your abilities, so be careful."

Saylor let his eyes flick from one face to another, holding each for just a moment before moving on.

"I can't stress this enough. Be safe. All right?"

The assembled group muttered assent.

"Okay," Saylor said. "Then if no one has anything else, let's hit it."

***

Katie MacLeod wrote the traffic citation. Her pen skipped through the boxes, filling them out almost without thought. The driver had failed to stop for a red light and narrowly missed colliding with another car in the middle of the intersection. Katie had briefly considered arresting him for reckless driving, but the driver was immediately apologetic and obviously shaken up. A ticket for the red light violation would be enough.

As she wrote, Katie glanced up and around every few seconds. While this vigilance may have seemed extreme to the civilian onlooker, it had become second nature for her. Inattention was the number one reason officers got killed. A bit of caution went a long way.

Cautious like last night, Katie?

She exhaled deeply. That had been scary, running through the darkness after a guy with a gun. Then hearing shots ring out, not knowing if he was shooting back at her. She remembered how frightened and detached she had been at the same time, and how the roof of her mouth had itched strangely.

Katie took another deep breath. She filled in the Municipal Code for the red light violation and the fine. Images of the dark construction yard flashed through her mind. She shut them off and exited the car.

At the offender's vehicle, she stood behind the doorpost. The driver was leaning forward with his forehead resting on the steering wheel. He didn't notice her presence.

"Sir?"

The driver sat up immediately and turned to face her. Her positioning forced him to look over his own shoulder.

"Yes, officer?"

"Sir, what I have for you here is a citation for failing to stop for a steady red light. I need you to sign here," she pointed. "Your signature is not an admission of guilt, merely a promise to respond."

She handed him the pen and noticed his hand shook as he took it and signed his name.

"I'm so sorry, officer," he said as he handed the pen back.

Katie nodded. "I can see that, sir. That's why I didn't arrest you for reckless driving."

"I appreciate that."

Katie tore off his copy of the ticket and handed it to him. "Instructions on how to respond are on the back. You have fifteen days. Do you have any questions?"

The driver shook his head. "No, ma'am."

Katie gave him a nod and returned to her vehicle. Out of habit, she kept her eye on the offending vehicle as she did so. The driver signaled carefully and pulled back into traffic.

As she reached her own vehicle, a man approached her from the sidewalk. She watched him carefully.

"Can I help you, sir?"

The man lifted the bill of his baseball cap and nodded. "Yeah. I was in the car that guy almost hit. I was wondering, does he have any insurance?"

Katie paused. "Did he cause you to run into something?" She hadn't seen any collision, but maybe she missed something.

"No," he said, shaking his head. "But he scared me half to death. Does he have insurance?"

"He did," Katie told him.

"Can I get the policy number?"

Katie struggled not to show her disbelief. "Sir, there was no accident. He ran a red light and was cited for that."

"He ran a red light and almost killed me is what happened!"

Katie nodded her understanding. "And I will put exactly what happened in my report."

"You will?"

"Absolutely."

The man gave a tug on his cap, considered a

moment, then said in a subdued voice, "Well, okay then. But people like that shouldn't have a license!"

"You're probably right."

He watched her for moment before shrugging. "All right then."

"Have a nice night."

The man paused again, looking at her. He tugged his cap, adjusted his belt-line, then turned and walked back toward his car.

Katie wondered what she would find if she checked his license status. He was probably in suspended status. She cleared her traffic stop with the code One-Henry (citation issued) and started thinking about a nice cold Pepsi.

The convenience store at Monroe and Alvarado was considered officer-friendly. Katie pulled into the lot and backed her car into a parking place near the door. She turned her portable radio on as she got out of the car. Since she only planned on being a few minutes, she decided not to check out with radio. It was none of their business that she needed a drink.

Patrons stared as she entered the store. She could read their minds from the looks on their faces. *A woman cop?* After almost three years on the job, Katie had grown used to it. Some people were just surprised, others resentful, and some people found it amusing. She had been in several situations where a male suspect did not think she was serious about arresting him. He found out differently, even if it took baton strikes or pepper mace.

"The tools of my trade don't care about the gender of the hands that use them," she was fond of saying after the suspect-now-arrestee was put into the back of a patrol car.

From the cooler, Katie selected a large bottle of Pepsi and approached the counter.

"Adam-114, Adam-116."

"Adam-114, Regal and Olympic." Matt Westboard, a five-year veteran, answered with his location.

Katie answered up, knowing now that everyone listening to the north side channel would know she was on portable and hadn't checked out. *Oh, well.*

"A D-V, 2711 N. Waterbury. Complainant lives next door. Says he hears a male and female voice yelling and it sounds violent. The house comes back to a Marc Elliot and Julie Phillips. Checking both names now. 2711 N. Waterbury."

Katie copied the transmission, set down the Pepsi and hurried to her car. She ignored the fascinated patrons who watched her go. She was only a few blocks away from the house. She knew Matt was a ways off, but that shouldn't matter. Always the frustrated NASCAR driver, he'd make good time.

Katie shot out of the lot with her lights flashing and cut onto a side street. At Howard, one block before Waterbury, she swung north and traveled parallel to the 2700 block. 2711 would be on the west side of the street, she knew, so she parked just west of Waterbury, out of sight.

"Adam-116, on scene," she told radio.

Exiting the car, she slid her side-handle baton into its holder and walked south through the front yards until she reached 2711, third house from the corner. Frenzied yelling came from inside. The hair on the back of her neck stood up. The reassuring tap of her baton against the back of her leg and the comfortable weight on her right hip provided welcome reassurance.

A huge tree stood off-center in the yard and Katie took up a position behind it. Thank God for all the trees in River City. Not only were they beautiful, but they made excellent cover and concealment.

The screaming and yelling continued. Katie listened carefully but heard only words that she couldn't make out and some crying. From the sound of things, nothing was being broken. It didn't sound like an ongoing assault, either. Of course, she reminded herself, that didn't mean it hadn't already happened or wouldn't still happen.

"Adam-116 and -114, Marc Elliot is in with a misdemeanor warrant, which has been confirmed. He has an extensive record, including two convictions for Domestic Violence assault and several controlled substance entries. Phillips is in locally, no wants."

So we'll be arresting him no matter what, Katie thought pleasantly. The way he was screaming at her, he needed to go to jail.

Katie listened for another long minute before she

heard a female voice scream, "No, Marc, I'm sorry!" A scream of pain followed, though she heard no sound of strikes.

She clenched her teeth and debated whether or not to go in alone. Matt was probably less than a minute away. Still, a minute in a fight is an eternity. Hart's admonition following her lone pursuit of the guy through the construction yard still rang in her ears.

But if this woman's been hurt...

Her decision became moot as Marc Elliot burst out the front door and hurried down the steps. In the glaring porch light, she could see that his hands were covered in dark red. Blood splattered his face and shirt. Katie immediately spotted a long hunting knife in his right hand. She drew her weapon and pointed it at him.

"Police, don't move!"

Elliot turned slowly to face her. His face seemed askew and even at the distance of seven yards, she could see the craziness in his eyes.

"Put the knife down! Now!"

Elliot continued to stare at her.

Katie keyed her shoulder mike with her left hand. "Adam-116, have him step it up."

"Copy. Adam-114, step it up. Adam-113?"

"-13, responding."

"Adam-116." Katie's breathing quickened.

"Go ahead."

"I've got the male half here at gunpoint. He's bloody and armed with a large knife."

"Copy."

"I said put the weapon down!" Katie ordered again. She found herself wishing for that cold Pepsi.

Elliot's trance-like stare ended and his face slowly broke into a grin. "I am going to carve you up, bitch." He took a step toward her.

"Drop it!" she said, but her voice broke.

Elliot took another step. His smile widened.

Oh God, she thought, *I'm going to have to kill him.*

In all the fights she'd been in, she could never remember thinking that someone would die. Wrestle, punch, kick, get pepper-maced, but not die. She felt a stab of fear in her stomach as adrenaline washed over her. The roof of her mouth itched and beads of sweat popped out on her brow. For a moment, she thought she could smell freshly cut lumber. In the distance, she heard a car door shut.

Elliot took two more steps, reminding her of a lunatic Elmer Fudd. "Be vewwy quiet..." She almost gave into hysterical laughter at the thought.

Concentrate, goddamn it!

"Stop right there! Drop your weapon or I will shoot!"

Elliot chuckled and waved the knife. "Shoot, bitch. Shoot, you fucking bitch. Shoot me. Shoot me. Shootme, shootme!" He tapped his chest with handle of the knife. "C'mon, you stinking gash! Fucking woman cop slit!"

Katie barely heard the crude insults. She moved her finger from its indexed position into the trigger guard and onto the trigger. She would have to kill him.

"*Adam-116, an update,*" came the dispatcher's voice. Katie ignored the transmission and placed her front sight in the center of Elliot's chest.

"Come on, you whore. Shoot me!"

Could she?

"I don't want to shoot you," she said gently, hoping to talk him down. "Just put the knife down."

Elliot took her tactic as a sign of weakness. His manic grin melted into a mean glare, his teeth gritting hard. "I am going to cut you up, bitch. I am going to stick this knife in your—"

Elliot stopped and flinched, waving the knife at his eye as if brushing away a fly. A small red dot was dancing in his eyes.

"Over here." The voice was flat and deadly.

Elliot looked to his left. Katie followed his gaze

and saw Matt Westboard behind a car, his pistol pointed at Elliot's head.

Matt tickled Elliot's crazy eyes again with the laser sight then moved the small red dot down to his chest.

"You take one more step, motherfucker," Westboard told him, "and you are a dead man."

***

Officer Stefan Kopriva swung the car around the corner as if it were on rails, the roar of the big-block engine loud enough to pierce the sound of his siren as he powered down Utah Street.

"Adam-116, an update." The calm in the dispatcher's voice contrasted with Katie's moments earlier.

Kopriva whipped through the s-curves and cut the wheel hard to the right, turning onto Foothills Drive. He buried the accelerator.

"Adam-116 or Adam-114, an update."

C'mon, Katie, Kopriva thought, his knuckles white, his forearms rigid as he approached Ruby.

"Answer up," he whispered. He slowed briefly for the flashing red light at Ruby, checking left for traffic. There were two cars. Both slowed and pulled to the side. He pushed his air horn and blasted through the intersection.

"Adam-114, one in custody, code four."

"Copy. Code Four, one in custody at 2314 hours."

Kopriva shut off his siren and let loose a long sigh. He continued on to the scene in case they needed any help.

As he drove, he flexed his fingers and his forearms, working out the tension.

***

Arrest Report: Elliot, Marc.

Arresting Officer: Katie MacLeod, Badge #407

Charge(s): 1st Degree Assault with a Deadly Weapon (Domestic Violence), Possession of a Controlled Substance, Possession of Drug Paraphernalia, Warrant Arrest.

Page: 2 of 2

Continued from page 1

> heard screaming from within the residence. I could identify one distinct female and one distinct male voice. I then heard a female voice scream in pain and say, "No, Marc, I'm sorry."
>
> Suspect Elliot exited the house holding a large knife. There was blood on the knife and his hand. Blood was also splattered on his shirt and face.
>
> I identified myself as a police officer and ordered Elliot not to move. He complied. I then ordered him to drop the knife. He

refused, threatening to cut me with it. I ordered him repeatedly to drop the weapon, but he refused. He began advancing toward my position, asking me to shoot him. He called me several crude names.

Officer Westboard arrived on scene. Both he and I ordered the Suspect to stop. He finally complied and was ordered prone and handcuffed. I informed Suspect he was under arrest for a warrant, which radio had confirmed prior to my arrival on scene. Suspect was searched. In his right front pocket, I found a marijuana pipe with residue. In his left front shirt pocket, I found a small bindle of a brown substance that tested positive for methamphetamine.

Officer Westboard and Officer Kopriva cleared the house and informed me that Victim Phillips had lacerations to her arm and abdomen that were consistent with a knife wound. See Officer Westboard's report for information regarding the assault charge.

Medics arrived to treat Phillips. Suspect was placed in my patrol car and transported to jail, where he was booked for all three charges. The warrant, which was for driving with a suspended license, was read to him (see attached) and he was booked on the warrant.

I placed knife (item #1), drugs (#2) and MJ pipe (#3) on the property book. I requested a lab test for the drugs.

Ofcr. Katie MacLeod, badge #407

James Mace rose sluggishly from the couch. His entire body felt itchy. He scratched the side of his face. The stubble there had turned into a short beard. Sleep crust cascaded from his eyes as he rubbed them.

He glanced at the easy chair. Leslie lay curled into a ball with a blanket tossed over her. Where was Andrea? He lumbered to his feet and poked his head in the bedroom, only a few short paces from the living room in their small apartment. He saw her dirty blonde hair splayed across the pillow. She wore no clothing and used no blankets. He admired the curve of her back and buttocks, but averted his eyes before his gaze reached the needle marks on the back of her knees.

He plodded to the kitchen and opened the refrigerator. He stared at the wet, brownish leaves on a head of rotting lettuce. He wasn't hungry, anyway, but you'd think with two women in the house, the place would be cleaner and there might be a few groceries in the cupboard.

Mace chuckled, a rasping cough that sounded decades older than his twenty-seven years. *If his Army buddies could see him now*. They used to tease him about being a virgin until after he turned twenty-one. Well, he took care of that on their first trip overseas.

They'd shut their faces now, wouldn't they? He lived with two women and was balling both of them. And they both knew it. That had to top anything those guys ever did. Besides, they were squares for the most part, just drinking and women for them. They'd been afraid of the opium dens in Thailand. Mace hadn't been.

The goddamn Army, anyway. Since when did you give elite troops like the Rangers a piss test? They accepted his claim of having eaten poppy-seed cake at the first failure. After the second one, his CO ordered him not to eat poppy-seed cake ever again. His third failure resulted in a dishonorable discharge. They had offered him that or a court-martial. It wasn't much of an offer, but Mace recognized a parachute when he saw one.

So now what did he have for five years of service? No pension, his meager savings wiped out six months ago. His only trophy: a nice machete wound in the face, courtesy of a rebel in Panama.

Mace slammed the fridge door. Leslie stirred in her sleep. He stared at her. She was attractive, or had been, but still no match for Andrea. Or wasn't, before Andrea went to hell.

He needed a drink of water. Filling a plastic cup from Taco Bell with water, he allowed himself to gloat in his status as stud. How many men had two women? He did.

The tap water had a coppery taste to it and after only a couple of swallows he felt nauseous. He dumped the rest.

The couch beckoned to him. He flopped onto it and stared at the textured ceiling. He'd met Andrea before his hair even grew out after his discharge.

She'd proved to be the perfect medicine, accepting where others had rejected him. She soothed his pain over the Army, his family, everything. Definitely the best lay he'd ever had, and she knew where to find the good stuff.

He remembered how firm and luscious her body had been the first time he'd had her. So supple and willing. Over the months, though, it had deteriorated rapidly. Her breasts sagged, her athletic frame shriveled, and sores broke out. And, of course, the track marks.

They'd met Leslie at a party. No one would sell them anything until he started dancing with Leslie and kissing her. Andrea hadn't minded once he told her Leslie knew somebody who was holding.

Leslie got the 'H' and they left. He remembered feeling excited about sex for the first time in months as they drove to the apartment. When they arrived and all three fell into the bed before shooting up, he could hardly believe his luck. *What a wild night!*

So Leslie stayed. And for a while, it was great, but now, both of them were junkies. They couldn't control their habit. Instead, it controlled them. He could thank the Army for one thing: discipline.

Mace decided to take advantage of the fact that both women were sleeping. He went to the cabinet where he stored his works—and found the baggie empty beside the leather holder. He stared at it for a long moment, disbelieving, as if his gaze would cause the missing heroin to somehow materialize.

Fucking *bitches!* They raided his shit.

He flew across the room at Leslie, slapping her as hard as he could. The force of the blow knocked her from the chair to the floor where she lay, staring at him, blinking stupidly.

"You stealing, worthless bitch!" he shouted, slapping and punching without mercy. She covered her head with her hands, absorbing the blows without a sound.

Mace turned and headed for the bedroom. His rage subsided but his body had started to itch and shake. Nausea swept over him, even though he knew it was too soon for that. He had to get some more.

He shouldered through the bedroom door. Andrea sat on the bed, staring at him, her breasts exposed, the small tuft of hair below her belly clearly visible. The vision held no interest for him.

"Do you have any money left from your welfare check?" He asked her.

She shook her head.

"Any cash at all?"

Another shake.

No use asking Leslie, he thought. She wouldn't have raided his shit if she had money.

He studied Andrea and knew immediately she'd be no good, too strung out to help him. That was the way of it, lately. She wouldn't help, couldn't help, but she'd be there for her share when the goodies arrived.

"Leslie?"

No answer.

"Leslie? Don't make me come out there."

"What?" she replied sullenly.

"Are you cool? Can you drive?"

"I can drive."

Mace opened the bottom drawer of his dresser and withdrew a long black wig and a .38 revolver. Wordlessly, Andrea watched him, a dull stare in her eyes. Mace felt a stab of pity for her.

"Be back soon, baby. Be back with some medicine for what ails ya." He tried to smile.

Andrea smiled back, small and child-like.

Mace called for Leslie and they left.

Friday, August 16th
Graveyard Shift

Television. Thomas Chisolm sighed. *The world's most worthless invention.*

Fifty-seven cable channels, including movie channels, and yet he sat staring at the guide channel because he liked the music they were playing. Always a classic rock fan, before it was considered classic, Chisolm had slowly drifted towards country music over the past several years.

He drank a cold bottle of Coors. On his workdays, he rarely touched a drop of alcohol, but his night off, he sometimes had a few. Tonight, he'd made a considerable dent in the beer left over from the last shift party six weeks ago. He managed to achieve a steady buzz over the last couple of hours and now he'd hit his stride. The proper rate of consumption would keep him at this level of drunkenness without advancing or retreating for several more hours.

Goddamn Hart, Chisolm grated inwardly. He raised his bottle in mock tribute. "Here's to you, Lt. Alan Hart. Screw you, you pencil-necked prick." He took a hearty swig of the cold-filtered brew. *Good stuff.*

Hell, Hart wouldn't have lasted a week in Vietnam. Never would've made it through Special Forces training, the pansy. Probably'd gone crying home to his mommy inside of three days. Even if by some miracle, he'd made it through the training, once in the bush, a prick like that would have gotten fragged by his own men inside of a week.

Vietnam. Chisolm sipped his Coors and shook his head. How alive he'd been then. And how dead.

"The police department has some unrealistic expectations on how to deal with crime," he lectured the television. "We are too nice. Criminals don't respect that. They view it as weakness."

Chisolm twirled the bottle, watching it turn and wobble on the coffee table. "As police officers, we're expected to clean up crime. But our hands are tied." He shook his head. In 'Nam, his company had free rein to do whatever it took to flush the Viet Cong out of their sector. His CO took the hard line. If they even *suspected* someone of so much as lighting a cigarette for the VC, it was lights out for that poor sonofabitch.

Captain Mack Greene. Now that had been a commanding officer. Hart looked like a little boy sucking his thumb next to Captain Greene. About the only River City officer that came close to Greene on the department was Lieutenant Robert Saylor, Chisolm's lieutenant on graveyard.

He wondered briefly if he should talk to Saylor about Hart, then dismissed the idea. Hart oversaw the FTO program. No use going to Saylor. Besides, Chisolm wasn't about to whine to his superiors about something as inconsequential as Alan Hart.

"Fuck," Chisolm whispered for no specific reason, repeating his father's favorite curse phrase. "Fuck a duck and make it cluck."

He glanced at the letter on his kitchen counter,

where it had sat for a month. The ragged edges where he'd torn open the envelope stared back at him.

The letter came from his sister in Portland. She'd written to tell him that Sylvia had gotten married. She wondered if he had known.

Chisolm sighed heavily. He often wished he hadn't blown things with Sylvia, but it wasn't until that letter arrived that he realized how deeply those wishes went.

Well, if wishes were horses, beggars would ride. He smiled bitterly. *And if worms had .45's, birds wouldn't mess with them.*

After receiving the letter, he'd promptly gone to Duke's, picked up a twenty-year-old cop groupie, brought her home and nailed her. Afterward, he found himself wondering if his pulse had even quickened during the entire affair.

Sylvia had dignity, and with his reaction to her recent marriage, he'd proven he had none.

Chisolm finished the bottle and strode to the fridge to get another. The bottle hissed slightly as he twisted the top off. She got married. So what? She left River City five years ago. What did he want her to do? Brood forever, like him?

The television guide channel suddenly annoyed him. He grabbed the remote flicked the off button.

"You know," he said to the small pinpoint of light on the TV screen, "the thing that bothers me the most about losing the FTO gig is that I am good for those kids. They come out of the Academy and can barely tell the difference between a bad guy and a magpie. I teach them what they need to survive. Other FTO's teach them other things." He jabbed his index finger at the TV to stress each word. "But I concentrate on how to stay alive. How to be a warrior in peace-time."

Just like in 'Nam. Try to show them enough to stay alive, so their deaths aren't on your conscience.

But Thomas Chisolm housed a vast cemetery in his conscience and all the beer in the fridge wasn't going to wash it away.

**

River City PD had a successful Reserve Officer program. Reserves were subjected to the same hiring process as commissioned officers and then attended a condensed version of the Police Academy. They always rode with a commissioned officer, except for a handful that graduated to a higher rank and rode in two-man reserve cars. They were all volunteers.

Some officers resented the reserves, claiming their presence took the place of hiring another commissioned officer. Stefan Kopriva disagreed. He saw the reserves as a supplement, not a replacement.

Besides, Kopriva knew that the same people who complained about the reserves taking away jobs would grouse even louder if they had to field some of the calls reserves often took. Reserves fielded a steady diet of cold burglary reports, bicycle thefts, and found property calls, all things most cops considered boring.

The Reserve Officer in Kopriva's car was a green

one, just three rides out of the Academy. Kopriva didn't mind. The kid seemed bright and eager to learn. Kopriva had discovered something in his *sensei's* karate *dojo*. He'd found it gave him satisfaction to show someone a skill and then see that person 'get it.' Police work, sometimes a very play-it-by-ear profession with a lot of gray area, was tricky to actually teach someone and thus, even more gratifying when someone caught on.

Kopriva let the reserve, Ken Travis, drive for the first half of the shift until oh-one-hundred. Then they switched. Not surprisingly, none of the officers in his previous three rides had allowed him to drive.

"Were they from the sit down and shut up school of thought?" he asked.

Travis nodded. "Pretty much. But you learn a lot from watching."

"Not as much as from doing," Kopriva said.

Ten minutes later, Kopriva spotted a maggot car sneaking down Regal, a side street with a lot of offsetting intersections. This allowed drivers to treat it like an arterial. Frequently, drivers without a valid license used it, a practice so common that Kopriva and his sector-mates had dubbed any car on Regal after midnight in violation of the "felony Regal law."

Kopriva pulled in behind the car, a Monte Carlo, about a '71 or '72. "Find the stop," he instructed Travis. He'd already noticed the driver's side headlight was out, an Easter Egg of a stop. The vehicle sped along thirty miles per hour, five over the limit. And to make things even easier, the passenger-side taillight was broken and showing white light to the rear.

Travis peered at the car for a block. In that time, the vehicle slowed to twenty-three miles per hour.

"How fast is he going?" Travis asked him.

"Twenty-three, twenty-four now."

He stared at the car for another long moment, then saw it. "Broken tail-light?"

"Are you asking me or telling me?" Kopriva asked good-naturedly.

"Telling."

"Do we stop them?"

Travis didn't hesitate. "Yes."

Kopriva picked up the mike. Before notifying radio, he told Travis, "There's two of them. If one runs, stay with the car. If both run, you take the passenger. Okay?"

Travis nodded, his eyes dancing with excitement.

Kopriva recited the license plate and their location to radio and activated his overhead lights. The car immediately pulled to the side while Kopriva put his spotlight and takedown lights on the vehicle. He slammed the car into park and still managed to beat Travis out of the car.

Both occupants remained seated, neither one seat-belted. Kopriva approached cautiously, lighting up the back seat with his heavy mag light and then searching for the driver's hands. They were on the wheel. The passenger's hands rested on his lap.

"Is there a problem, officer?" asked the driver, a white male in his mid-twenties with long, greasy hair and a scraggly growth of beard.

Typical maggot.

"You have several equipment defects, sir. Your headlight is out and one tail-light is broken."

"They are?" The driver acted surprised.

Kopriva nodded. "You were also traveling at thirty miles per hour. The speed limit here is twenty-five."

"I thought it was thirty."

"It's twenty-five. May I see your driver's license, registration and proof of insurance?"

"Yes, sir." The driver began to dig through a pile of papers above the visor.

Kopriva motioned over the top of the car to Travis, who stood by the passenger window. "Get his I.D."

Travis nodded and spoke to the passenger.

The driver nervously handed Kopriva an insurance card that had expired four months ago, along with the registration. The registered owner was Pete Maxwell.

"Are you Pete?"

The driver shook his head. "No. Pete's my friend. He loaned me the car." He handed Kopriva his license.

Kopriva looked at it. Right away, he noticed it was a state identification card, not a license. While a perfectly legal form of identification, even issued by Department of Licensing, it was not a license.

"Well, Mr..." Kopriva glanced at the card. "Mr. Rousse. This is not a license. Do you have a license?"

Rousse shook his head. "It's suspended," he said ruefully.

"And Mr. Maxwell's insurance has lapsed."

Rousse nodded glumly.

"Okay, wait here. I'll be back in a minute." Kopriva glanced at Travis. "Got his I.D.?"

Travis shook his head. "He won't give it to me."

Oh *really*? Kopriva peered at the passenger through the driver's window. "What's your name?"

The man had jet-black hair, shaved on the sides and long in the back. His beard stubble was thick. He stared straight ahead and didn't respond to Kopriva's question.

"I said, what's your name, passenger!" Kopriva put an edge in his voice.

The man turned. "Why do I have to tell you?"

He has a warrant.

"Are you wearing a seat-belt?" Kopriva asked.

"No. Well, I was. I took it off when we stopped."

Kopriva shook his head. "No, you didn't. You weren't wearing one. That's a traffic infraction. You are now required to identify yourself. If you don't, I'll arrest you for Refusal To Cooperate. Now what's your name?"

The passenger considered briefly, then said, "I'm Dennis Maxwell."

Travis wrote it in his pocket notebook.

"Middle initial?" Kopriva asked.

"G."

"Date of birth?"

"Uh, ten...seventeen, sixty-three. I mean, sixty-two." He gave a nervous grin. "Listen, I'm not trying to be a jerk. I've just been hassled by cops in the past."

"I'm not hassling you," Kopriva stated coldly. "I'm doing my job."

Dennis nodded. "Yeah, all right. Sorry."

"No problem," Kopriva said. As he walked back to the car, he muttered, "You lying, lying, *lying* bag of crap."

Back in the car, Kopriva switched to the data channel so Travis could run both names. "Get physicals on Maxwell. And have them run the registered owner, too."

The data channel was busy and the dispatcher took forever to respond with their requested information. Kopriva wondered when they would get the computers in the patrol car. While they waited, he quizzed Travis on all the infractions they could write Rousse for. The reserve did well on his answers.

"What about the passenger?" Kopriva asked him.

"Kind of a jerk," Travis said.

"You think he's telling the truth?"

Travis shrugged. "I suppose. He just doesn't like the police."

Kopriva suppressed a smile. Three years ago, he would have thought the same thing. Now he knew better.

Travis had almost finished writing the infractions before radio called out for Baker-123. Kopriva ignored it, giving Travis a chance to answer. On the second call, he picked up the mike himself.

"Baker-123, go ahead."

"Rousse is in locally, extensive record, but no current wants. DOL is suspended for refusing the breath test. Also."

"Go ahead."

"Bravo-123."

Kopriva felt a stab of anger. The code was designed to inform the police officer that one of the subjects being checked had a warrant. Calling the unit by the military alphanumeric ensured that if the suspect were in earshot, he would not inadvertently overhear traffic.

"Go ahead, I'm clear for traffic," he told radio, keeping his tone neutral. The dispatcher should have told him about the warrant first, not in the order he gave the names. But his anger quickly washed away with the satisfaction of having been right.

"It's for Maxwell, Pete, your RO. $2,030 bond on a misdemeanor drug charge. He's five-ten, one-fifty, black hair, brown eyes. Also."

"Have records confirm the warrant. Go ahead your also."

"Maxwell, Dennis G. in locally, no wants. He's six-two, two-hundred thirty, blond and blue."

"Copy, thanks." Kopriva replaced the mike and turned to Travis, who sat open-mouthed throughout the exchange. "Now, what do we have?"

Travis thought for a moment. "Well, the driver's suspended, so we write him for that."

Kopriva nodded. "What else?"

"The registered owner has a warrant."

Kopriva waited for a long minute, giving Travis a chance to think some more. Travis furrowed his brow, but said nothing.

"Did the passenger have hard I.D.?" Kopriva finally asked.

"No."

"Is he six-two?"

"I don't know. Maybe." Travis started to squirm.

Kopriva shrugged. "Maybe," he said easily. "Hard to tell when someone is sitting down. Did he look like he weighed two-thirty? Did he have blonde hair?"

Realization flooded Ken Travis' face. "He's not Dennis. He's Pete."

Kopriva nodded. "Exactly. He is probably Pete, the registered owner. He has a warrant, so he decided to play the name game. Only he's not very good at it. He picked Dennis, probably his brother or a cousin, whose physicals don't even come close."

"Not too smart," Travis observed.

"Hey, these people aren't rocket scientists. Thank God."

Travis chuckled.

Kopriva continued, "So now what do we do?"

"Arrest him."

Kopriva gave a slow half-nod. "Well, yes. But first we get confirmation from records through radio. And let's cut a ticket for Rousse on his suspended driving. Do we know for sure that this passenger is Pete?"

"Not for sure, no."

"So we play the name game back and we get confirmation. Leave that to me. Then we arrest him. After the arrest, then what?"

"We give Rousse his tickets?"

Kopriva smiled. "We'll do that first. Travis, don't be afraid to be wrong. Tell me, don't ask. It's okay to make a mistake."

Travis nodded several times. "Okay. After the arrest, we take him to jail."

"True, but first we get to do something. What?"

Travis paused, thinking. Then he smiled. "We get to search the car."

"Why?"

"Search incident to an arrest." His smile broadened. "If the arrest is made out of a vehicle, officers may search the vehicle."

"Excellent. Now finish those tickets. I'll keep an eye on our little misdemeanant."

Travis wrote quickly, obviously enthused. Kopriva felt the same way. His job was like a puzzle sometimes. Fit in who was who, figure out the truth, the partial truth and the lies. Then make the call.

"Baker-123, warrant is confirmed."

"Copy. Have records hold it."

Travis finished the tickets and they stepped out of the patrol car. Kopriva called Rousse back to the car, directing him to stand at the push-bar in the center of the front bumper. He kept the front corner of the vehicle between himself and Rousse.

"Mr. Rousse," he said, placing the tickets on the hood of the car, "I am citing you tonight." He explained each of the tickets and directed him where to sign. Rousse cooperated and didn't appear angry. Once he'd signed the ticket, Kopriva tore off his copies and handed them to him.

"Mr. Rousse, what is your passenger's name?"

Rousse's eyes flitted nervously from the car to Kopriva and back again. "Dennis. Dennis Maxwell."

"And where's Pete tonight?"

"Home, I guess."

"What is Pete to Dennis?"

"His brother."

Kopriva stared at Rousse. "Why are you lying for him, Mr. Rousse?"

"I'm not. His name is Dennis. Honest, you can ask

him."

"Okay, if that's how you want it." Kopriva pointed. "Go back to your car, put your hands on the steering wheel and stay there."

Rousse obeyed. As the driver reached the car, Kopriva called to the passenger. "Dennis, come back here for a minute."

Dennis obeyed. Kopriva half-expected him to run, but evidently he had faith in his name ruse. Kopriva almost laughed in disgust as he watched a black-haired male about five-ten and one-hundred-fifty pounds approach his car.

"Stand right there by my push-bar, please."

Dennis complied, crossing his arms.

Kopriva eyed him for a full minute until Dennis finally raised his hands questioningly, "What?"

"Why are you lying to me, Dennis?"

"I'm not."

"Yes, you are," Kopriva said with a nod. "Do I look like an idiot to you?"

"No," Dennis answered quietly.

"Did I forget to erase the STUPID stamp off my forehead before shift tonight?"

"What's the problem?"

"The problem is, you're not Dennis. You're not

even close. What's more, you look a lot like Pete Maxwell. Now can you explain that to me?"

"I am Dennis Maxwell."

"What do you weigh?"

"One-seventy or so. But I lost a lot of weight in the last few months. I used to weigh almost two-forty. I was fat." Sweat collected on his upper lip and he fidgeted from foot to foot.

"And I suppose you dyed your hair black, too, huh?" Kopriva's voice dripped with sarcasm.

Dennis nodded.

"And what? Shaved off three inches from the soles of your feet?" Kopriva shook his head in disgust. "Uh-uh. Don't insult my intelligence. You're Pete Maxwell."

"I am Dennis. Swear to God."

Kopriva looked at Travis. The reserve stood enthralled by the entire exchange. Kopriva winked, then stepped around the car and leaned toward the fidgeting, sweating suspect. "Okay, *Dennis,* I'll tell you what I am going to do. First, I'll call for another unit to go to the station and get a printout photo of you and your brother. He'll bring those pictures up here while I detain you. See, Pete has a warrant for his arrest. So when my friends get here and show me the pictures and you mysteriously look like Pete and not anything like Dennis, that's when I place you under arrest for the warrant."

Dennis squirmed, then opened his mouth to speak.

Kopriva raised his finger to cut off his denial, "Not only that, I will charge you for lying to me about your name in order to avoid arrest. Plus, I will arrest your friend for the same charge, since he is backing up your lie."

He gave Dennis a long stare. The suspect looked away and back again, shifting his stance from side to side.

"Now, if you save me from all that messing around and just admit who you really are and take care of your warrant like a man, I will only arrest you for the warrant. Nothing else." Kopriva shrugged. "Otherwise, you get it all, the whole enchilada. I'll even write you for no seatbelt."

A long minute of silence followed. The only sounds Kopriva could hear were the engine idling and the clicking and whirring of his overhead lights. Having played out his hand, he held Dennis' stare, showing him that it wasn't a bluff.

Dennis looked away and sighed heavily. "I'm Pete Maxwell. I've got I.D. in my back pocket."

"Pete, you're under arrest." Kopriva quickly cuffed and searched him. He found a marijuana pipe in Maxwell's right front pocket and placed it on the hood. He put the rest of his property into a plastic bag. Travis guided Pete into the back of the police car.

Kopriva called Rousse out of the car.

"Stand here," he said, pointing next to Travis at the front of the patrol car. Then he searched the car. In the center console, he found a small Tupperware container roughly the size of a fifty-cent piece. He opened it carefully and saw a brown chunky substance inside.

Meth.

The rest of his search turned up nothing. Kopriva retrieved a field test kit from the trunk of his car. The small plastic vials had ampules with chemicals in them that reacted with specific drugs by turning a particular color. He used his knife to slice off a sliver of the substance in the Tupperware container and dropped it in. When he broke the ampules, the test tube immediately flowed orange.

Positive.

Kopriva showed the tube to Travis.

"What's going on?" Rousse asked.

"You're under arrest for possession of methamphetamine," Kopriva told him, applying a mild wristlock. He motioned with his head for Travis to cuff Rousse.

"What's that?" the man asked unconvincingly.

"Crank," Kopriva told him. "Like you don't know."

"It's not mine," Rousse protested.

Kopriva searched him, finding nothing of importance. He requested another unit for transport. He sat Rousse down on the curb with his legs straight out in front of him. Travis stood guard behind him.

"Baker-123, is there a sergeant available?"

"L-123, go ahead."

Sgt. Shen, Adam sector sergeant. Good.

"L-123, can you contact me at Regal and Olympic?"

"Affirm, from Division and Wabash."

"Copy." So the Sarge was having coffee at Denny's with the Lieutenant. He shouldn't be too long.

A dark brown Chevy cruised past the traffic stop slowly. Too slowly. Kopriva broke the snap on his holster and rocked his pistol forward. The car looked familiar...

Isaiah Morris!

Morris was a gangbanger from Compton. He'd arrested the Crip about two months ago on a warrant and found crack cocaine stuffed into his sock. Not enough to prove Morris was dealing, but still a solid possession arrest.

Kopriva followed the car with his eyes. It rolled slowly by. Morris glared at him through the passenger window. Then the tires chirped and the car sped away. Kopriva switched to the data channel and ran Morris' name. He doubted that Morris had appeared on the drug charge. Maybe there was a warrant out for him.

While he waited, Kopriva decided to see if he could plant a seed. He picked up the marijuana pipe and opened the back door of the patrol car. "See this?" he asked Pete.

Pete nodded.

"Since you told me the truth, I'm going to dump it and not charge you. Next time I talk to you, don't lie to me."

"Thanks, man. I appreciate it."

"Don't thank me yet. I found Meth in your console."

Pete winced. "Can't you just dump the crank, too?"

Kopriva shook his head. "A pipe is one thing. Nobody cares too much. Drugs are something else. People care about drugs. It's a problem."

"Yeah," Pete said mournfully. "I know. My niece just went through D.A.R.E. at school."

"Then you get what I mean. Besides, my sergeant is coming here. I think he wants to charge both of you."

"What? Hey, that shit's not mine, man. It's his."

Kopriva held up his hand. "I'm sure it is, Pete. I'll try to talk him out of it, but this isn't my normal sergeant. This guy is kind of a hard ass about drugs. We'll see."

"All right," Pete said, resigned. "Thanks for chucking the pipe, man. Straight up."

"No problem."

Kopriva closed the door and walked to the sidewalk where a dutiful citizen had put out his garbage can. With a casual look around to satisfy no one was watching, he slipped the pipe into the garbage.

Rousse sat on the sidewalk curb, looking dejected and angry. Travis stood behind him.

Kopriva got his attention and asked, "Whose crank is that, anyways? You guys share?"

Rousse sniffed. "Nice try."

"Nice try what?"

"Whatever it is you found, it ain't mine. Just like I said. So you can save your little cop interrogation games, all right?"

Kopriva glanced at Travis. "He gets a little testy when things don't go his way, huh?"

Before Travis could answer, Rousse said, "Fuck you, man. I want to talk to my lawyer. His name is Joel Harrity."

Kopriva smiled. Harrity was a local defense attorney who crusaded against the police department. Most of the maggots who claimed him couldn't afford him.

"What're you smiling about, punk?" Rousse demanded. "I want to see your sergeant."

Kopriva shrugged. "People in hell want ice water. That don't mean they get it."

Rousse glared at him, then shook his head. "Whatever."

Baker-122 arrived. Officer Anthony Battaglia climbed out of the passenger side. His partner, Connor O'Sullivan, remained in the vehicle.

"What's up, Stef?" Battaglia asked.

"Got a warrant, found some meth in the car. That's the driver," he pointed to Rousse. "Can you transport him to jail for me? I'll be right behind you after I talk to Sgt. Shen."

"Sure." Battaglia waved O'Sullivan out of the car and they walked to where Travis guarded Rousse. Each officer took an arm and pulled Rousse to his feet. At their patrol car, O'Sullivan searched Rousse again. Kopriva didn't take offense, though he knew some officers did, which was too bad, in his opinion. If he put someone in his car, it was only after he searched them himself. He expected the same from other officers.

Once Rousse was stowed in the back of the patrol car, Battaglia waved to him and the pair headed south on Regal, slowing to talk momentarily with someone in another police car. Kopriva recognized it as the Sergeant's car. After a moment, O'Sullivan accelerated away and continued south.

Sgt. Miyamoto Shen pulled his car in behind Kopriva's and waited. Kopriva walked over and leaned into the window.

"What do you have, Stef?" the trim sergeant asked him.

"I stopped the car," Kopriva explained, "and the passenger played the name game. Once we got that straightened out, it turns out he has a warrant. He's the one in my car. Anyway, I found some meth in the console. Battaglia and Sully have my driver and they're running him in for me on the meth."

"So what do you need?"

"I want to do the weasel in the passenger seat, too. He's the registered owner. I'd like to arrest them both for constructive possession."

Shen considered. "So the driver is not the registered owner?"

"No."

"And the RO was in the passenger seat?"

"Yes."

"Where'd you find the drugs? The glove box?"

Kopriva shook his head. "No, the console between the seats. Both had access."

"What are they saying?"

Kopriva's radio crackled. *"Bravo-123."*

"Neither one has been read their rights, but both say it's the other guy's meth," he told Shen, then answered the radio. "Go ahead, I'm clear for traffic."

"Morris is in as a confirmed gang member. He has a felony want for possession of crack cocaine, bail is $25,000."

"Copy. I don't have him here. Also, have records ship over the warrant for Maxwell."

"Copy."

Kopriva explained to Shen, "Isaiah Morris drove by us while I was waiting for Sully and Battaglia. So, what do you think about these two here?"

Shen stroked his chin for a moment. "Do them both for constructive possession. Be detailed in your report on where you found the dope and the issue of access for both parties. Their statements, too."

"I will. Thanks."

"Good stop, Stef."

"Thanks."

Shen drove off. Kopriva locked the doors to the Monte Carlo and returned to his patrol car.

Maxwell leaned forward, his voice muffled by the plastic shield. "What'd he say?"

"He said I have to do you both. Sorry, man."

"Really?"

"Yep."

"Oh, man, I don't need this shit."

"Sorry."

"Shit. Well, thanks for trying, man. Thanks for the pipe, too."

Kopriva nodded. He turned on his favorite rock station and faded the music to the back. It kept the prisoners from hearing the conversation between the officers.

"Advise radio we are en route to jail with one and our mileage is reset." Kopriva punched the trip odometer reset. "And get our time of stop and a report number."

Travis advised radio and carefully noted the time and report number. "Wow," he said. "That was cool."

"That is the way the game is played. That suspended ticket we wrote Rousse? He likely won't appear on it, so it'll go to warrant. Next time he gets stopped, he gets arrested again and we get into his car and find his drugs again. Ba-da-boom, ba-da-bing."

Travis nodded his head, smiling.

"See," Kopriva continued, "some officers act like traffic enforcement is beneath them. But traffic is one of our best tools. Just because you stop someone doesn't mean you have to write them. I let people off all the time. Decent people. Sometimes even shitheads. But look what happened tonight. We stopped Rousse on a piddly traffic stop for defective equipment. Now we have a misdemeanor, a warrant and two felonies. Plus about three misdemeanors we threw away, if you count the pipe and obstructing charges."

"Great," Travis said. "This is great." He nodded his head to the music and grinned.

The two were quiet the rest of the way to jail. Kopriva thought about how he would like to catch Morris again. Cream's "Sunshine of Your Love" came on the radio. Kopriva turned it up.

"I've been waiting so long..."

Maxwell leaned forward and yelled over the din. "At least you guys got good tunes."

"To be where I'm going…"

"Rock-n-roll," Kopriva yelled back and flashed a grin at Travis. Pete Maxwell might be a doper maggot but now he thought they were buddies. You never knew when that might come in handy.

"In the sunshine of your luuhh-uuuhhve!"

They drove into the sally port at jail and secured their weapons in the lock-box outside the door. Kopriva walked Maxwell into the officer's booking area and O'Sullivan handed him a booking slip.

"Rousse is all done, except for the report number."

"Thanks, Sully."

Battaglia nudged Kopriva. "You better check his work. Sometimes he forgets and he writes shit in Gaelic."

"Better than Italian," O'Sullivan fired back. He shook his head at Kopriva. "I can't tell you how many times we've come in here to book someone named Mamma Mia."

"Hey!" Battaglia said. "Leave my mother alone."

O'Sullivan smiled. "Italian boys and their mothers."

"Irish boys and their dresses."

"They're kilts, not dresses."

Battaglia rolled his eyes and clapped Kopriva on the shoulder. "Good pinch, Stef."

The two officers left, tossing insults at each other on the way out the door.

Kopriva filled out the booking slip for Maxwell and completed Rousse's. A jailer brought out Maxwell's warrant. Kopriva told Travis to read it to Maxwell.

Officer James Kahn stood in the corner of the small booking area. He looked up from his paperwork at Kopriva. "What'd you get, hotshot?"

"Warrant. Some meth." Kahn was a hard-charger and Kopriva respected that. On the few calls he'd been on with him, though, Kahn had exhibited almost zero compassion. "What are you here for?"

Kahn cocked an eyebrow at him. "You know what's a bad day? It's a bad day when a policeman shows up at your doorstep at midnight with two Child Protective Services workers. He takes your kids and places them with CPS, then arrests you and your wife for warrants right out of your living room. That's a bad day, man."

Kopriva waited, knowing there was more to come.

"You know what's a good day?" Kahn asked. "It's a good day when you're a cop and CPS calls you to go to some meth maggot's house to place his kids in foster care. You go there and turn his kids over to CPS and then you arrest him and his skanky wife right out of their living room on some drug warrants. That is a good day."

Kopriva laughed. "A very good day."

Kahn returned to writing his report. Kopriva gathered up his own paperwork. The jailers returned their cuffs, they retrieved their weapons and left jail. It was still early enough to get into some more action.

Sunday August 18th
Graveyard Shift

Pyotr Ifganovich thanked the customer for his business as he handed over the change. He preferred to go by the English version of his name, Peter. At varying times, depending on the government in power, it had been a popular name in Russia.

Here in America, he'd discovered Peter had also once been a popular name. He had not been so foolish as to believe all the lies the Soviet government told the Russian people regarding this nation, once his enemy. Neither had he been naïve enough to believe the myths of unsurpassed riches whispered out of KGB earshot.

When he arrived in River City, he found some of both. Of course, it was the riches he noticed first. He recalled the first time he stood in a Safeway store and struggled not to weep at the shelves bulging with food, coffee and toilet paper. Yes, America was wealthy.

He quickly enrolled in English classes and studied for his citizenship along with Olga, his wife. Their son, four-year-old Pavel (they called him Paul now), didn't remember Minsk and as he grew older, his appreciation for America obviously did not mirror that of his parents. Now ten years old, Paul spoke English better than both his parents and without an accent.

America was good to him and his family. He could apply for any job he wanted and the best applicant usually got the job. His work as farmer in Minsk, didn't qualify him for many jobs here in America. The convenience store provided a great opportunity for him. More importantly, his son could go to an American school, learn English and become an American. Yes, America was good to him.

Of course, Peter saw some of the evils, too. Six years in this country and this was the best job he had been able to get so far. It paid just above minimum wage, with a few extra cents an hour for working the evening shift. Peter got off at eleven, in time to meet Olga at the bus stop and ride home. She worked cleaning rooms at a local motel.

Crime. That was the biggest difference he noticed between the two countries. Not language, philosophy or government. Crime. In Minsk, crime existed but as a subtle presence, if not outright rare. KGB and local police made sure of that. Penalties were severe. People still disappeared, even as of six years ago. Here in America, the justice system seemed almost worthless. People shoplifted all the time from the store where he worked, or did gas drive-offs, and nothing happened. Nothing could be done. He felt sorry for the police, who had to deal with the same criminals again and again. They caught them and the judges set them free. It was shameful. America was wealthy, but she had too much freedom.

Peter cleaned the counters around the register for the fifteenth or twentieth time that night. He took pride in his work. He hoped the store manager, a gaunt man with a red nose that reminded Peter of his Uncle Ivan, would notice and promote him to night manager. They could use the money.

He considered going to the supply closet to get the broom and sweep the floor when a customer entered. The man appeared shaken. Peter wondered if he had been involved in a car accident or something. Even though it was against the rules, he allowed people to use the business telephone for such things.

The customer's long black hair fluttered in the artificial breeze created by the closing door.

Peter started to smile a greeting, when the man shoved a dark gun in his face, touching him on the end of the nose. Peter's hands flew up instinctively.

"Give me the fucking money in the register. Now!"

Not taking his eyes off the man's face, his fingers fumbled with the register. The drawer slid open.

"All of it, in a bag. Let's go."

What a terrible scar, Peter thought absently, shoving bills into a plastic bag. Flat eyes, like those of a shark, peered out from beneath thick eyebrows. The lids beneath them twitched rapidly.

Cold realization knotted his gut: the man wanted to kill him.

"The money, man. Let's go!" The robber pressed the gun against his forehead.

It was then Peter remembered something from the newspaper. *This is Scarface.* He'd robbed almost a dozen stores.

Peter's heart raced and his thoughts turned dark. *Is he going to shoot me now? I can't afford a bed at the hospital.*

The man snatched the bag from his hand. He glared at Peter with the eyes of a predator. Peter wanted to close his eyes and pray, but he couldn't move. *I have come all the way from Russia to die in River City, Washington. How tragic. Dosteovsky would appreciate the irony.*

The man removed the barrel of the gun from Peter's forehead and pressed it roughly against his chin. A single, stoic tear slid down Peter's face as he waited. He now had the presence of mind to ask God silently to care for Olga and Paul.

The man paused half a breath, then pushed the barrel into Peter's chin again. He could see the man's finger twitch as it pressed against the trigger. He repeated his prayer quickly, hoping that God would hear it before he was killed.

Please, God. Care for my wife and child. Please, God—

In a rush, the man lowered the gun and ran from the store. The bell dinged to signal his parting.

Peter stood stock-still, wondering that he was alive and thanking God over and over again. He looked at the clock. 9:31 PM. Every moment from now on was a gift from God.

His gift was already two minutes old when he thought to push the robbery alarm button located under the register drawer.

***

Threes and sevens. Coffee breaks and meal breaks in police radio speak. Some days you lived for them.

Katie MacLeod sat with Matt Westboard, gingerly picking at her sub sandwich. Matt devoured half of his in two large bites. Their dinner so far had been a quiet one, radio chatter at a minimum on a slow graveyard shift. She commented on that.

Matt nodded as he took a long sip on his soda.

"Nothing like last week," she said. "Scarface. And Elliot."

Matt continued to nod and sip.

Jesus, Katie thought. *Is he ever going to breathe?* She picked up an olive and popped it in her mouth.

With a sigh, Matt came up for air. "That call was intense. That maggot had serious problems with women."

"Yeah. Especially me." Katie tried to be casual. "I thought I was going to have to shoot him."

"Might've had to. He was all jacked up on meth would be my bet. You found some on him, right?"

Katie nodded.

"You should have seen the girlfriend. He stabbed her three times." Westboard pointed at his own body, pantomiming the injuries. "Once in the arm and twice in the belly. She had some defensive wounds, too, on her hands. You know what she told me on the way to the hospital?"

"No. What?"

"That he didn't do it. She came up with some crazy story about a burglar." He shook his head in disgust and took another long draught of his soda.

Katie frowned. *Stupid woman.* Then she asked, "Did you think you were going to have to shoot?"

Matt met her eyes. She wondered if he could sense her inner doubt.

"It was a fifty-fifty chance," he said. "Either he had a problem with anybody there or he had a problem with you in particular. Given his attitude about women and the names he was calling you, I kinda figured he might listen to me."

"What if he hadn't?"

Matt smiled, but kept his eyes on hers. He formed a gun with his thumb and forefinger. "Little red dot." He dropped his thumb like a hammer. "Bang. Big red dot."

Katie gave a small smile. It didn't ease her doubt.

Matt took a huge bite of his sub sandwich. "Yu evah heah abow Huk?" he said with his mouth full.

"What?!"

Matt grinned while he chewed. She recognized his poor table manners were an act intended to lighten her mood.

He swallowed. "I said, did you ever hear about the guy they called Hulk?"

"No, not really. Wasn't he some guy that quit a year or so before I was hired?"

"Yeah. His name was Joe Grushko. Everyone called him Hulk because he went about six-four and easily two-fifty. Solid muscle. He still holds the bench-press record at the station gym. Anyway, you ever hear why he quit?"

Katie shook her head, not really interested. She picked absently at a piece of shredded lettuce.

Matt went on. "Hulk was not afraid of anything that I could see. Getting into a fight around him was like being front row at a WWF bout. Guys and furniture flying. *Everywhere*." He waved his arms for emphasis. "So one night, he goes on a suicidal with a gun call. They get to the house and there is this little five-foot, ninety-pound woman waving a Beretta nine-em-em around. Hulk had a dead drop on her when she pointed the gun at him, but he didn't fire. He said later that he couldn't do it."

"What happened?" Katie asked, her interest piqued.

"She capped off a round at him and missed. He still didn't return fire. You know Tom Chisolm, right?"

"Of course."

"Chisolm did her with the shotgun. One shot. Nearly ripped her in half." Matt leaned back in his chair. "Justified shooting, case closed. But Hulk turned in his badge."

Katie nodded but sighed inwardly. This did not exactly make her feel any better.

"You would have done it, Katie," Westboard said, his voice quiet but firm. "I saw your finger on the trigger, and I saw the steel in your eyes. I never doubted for a second that you would have dropped him."

Katie felt a tear well up and turned her head, wiping it away and composing herself. "I didn't want to," she muttered. She felt momentarily stupid for crying in front of Westboard. It was so... female. But it was better than talking to her boyfriend Kevin about it. At least Westboard understood the job. Kevin didn't.

"No one wants to," Westboard told her. "But you would have. Don't feel bad. Everyone wonders a little bit. Everyone. I wondered that day with Elliot. Hulk wondered. I'm sure Tom Chisolm wondered right before he blasted apart that woman who was shooting at another officer."

Katie turned back to face him, composed. She looked around the sandwich shop to see if anyone had noticed her moment of weakness.

"Don't second-guess yourself, Katie. You're a good cop. You'll always do what you have to do."

Katie took a deep breath and let it out, wanting to believe him. Knowing she should. Only time would tell. "It's just been a bad couple of days, is all." She shrugged. "First the deal with the robber and then that meth freak Elliot."

Westboard nodded, his eyes sympathetic. "When it rains, it pours."

The unmistakable sound of an alarm tone came

across both radios.

***

Lieutenant Alan Hart sat in his office, idly twirling his gold pen in his fingers. He'd worked late, ostensibly to catch up on FTO reports, but found himself lost in thought more often than not. After reading Payne's first weekly report since the transfer to Officer Glen Bates, he was pleased to see that the recruit's marks had increased noticeably over those Chisolm had given him.

Chisolm. What a burnout. Hart hated the way the man was so condescending toward him. *I'm a lieutenant!* Chisolm only had one stripe on his sleeve, making him a Patrolman First Class, an automatic promotion and basically just a pay raise over a slick-sleeved patrolman. No authority or extra duties. *What a loser.* Chisolm hadn't tested for promotion in fourteen years on the job. Yet he sauntered around, acting like the cat's meow.

Hart snorted. Well, he put that cat's meow in his place last week, hadn't he? And when Payne made probation, Hart's judgment over Chisolm's would be vindicated.

Some men were just not born to lead other men.

He stared absently at the promotion list for Captain. He'd heard rumors that Captain Rainey would retire before Thanksgiving. That opened up a slot. He occupied the number two position on the list, directly behind Lieutenant Robert Saylor.

Saylor. Hart's lip curled. Saylor liked Chisolm, which pretty much summed up Hart's opinion of him. He had no respect for any officer who curried favor with his troops.

Still, list position was only worth sixty percent on the promotions. Twenty percent went to seniority, negligibly in Hart's favor. The other twenty points were awarded by the patrol captain, based on performance reviews. He needed to find a way to impress the patrol captain. It was as simple as that.

Turning back to the FTO reports, Hart read about a brand new recruit named Willow. The radio, tuned to channel one, was turned down to the point of a whisper, but the high-pitched alarm tone came through clear. Hart turned up the radio.

"All units, hold-up alarm at 1643 E. Francis. Suspect is a single, white male, unknown clothing, long black hair, bearded, with a scar on left side of his face. Suspect displayed black handgun, then fled southbound on Pittsburg."

Hart cursed. That goddamn robber was making a mockery of River City PD. Twice this week, the local paper ran front-page stories on the department's seeming inability to nab Scarface.

"Units responding on Francis. Time delay is three minutes."

Hart cursed again, listening as the units drove into the area and set up a wide perimeter. A K-9 officer responded as well, but Hart knew it was useless. Too much of a delay.

Someone has to do something about this! He raged, then stopped suddenly.

Of course. Someone did.

He set aside Willow's report and put a yellow notepad in front of him.

Someone should form a task force and work tirelessly until Scarface was brought down. Someone like him. Someone who would be the next captain on this department.

Lt. Hart wrote feverishly, drafting a plan to submit to the patrol captain in the morning.

***

Anthony Giovanni sat at the bar, sipping his light beer. Duke's, essentially a cop bar, drew most of its business from off-duty or retired cops, their families and those who wanted to be around cops. This included some wannabes, usually coolly rebuffed. Others just hung out, never asking a cop to tell a story and frequently found themselves rewarded with a doozy. The clientele also included some badge bunnies, exactly what Gio was talking to at the moment.

She was a redhead, that soft strawberry hair rather than the wiry, copper color. Her green eyes caught his from the end of the bar almost forty minutes and a drink ago, and now they'd danced the pick-up waltz for a steady half-hour. She made the first sexual innuendo and after that, Gio set the hook.

When Johnny asked if they wanted another round, he looked at her questioningly.

"Okay," she said. "Unless you want to go somewhere else."

Gio glanced at the rise and fall of her bosom for a long second then met her eyes and flashed his best smile. "Just the tab, Johnny. Thanks."

He paid Johnny and tipped him well. Johnny always clued him in on the new bunnies, so Gio always took care of him. As he slid off the barstool, he found something was missing; he felt no excitement. This chesty, beautiful, redheaded woman had consented to go home with him, yet he found himself almost bored before it had even happened. The promise of her breasts seemed empty.

At the door, he brushed past a woman that stopped him dead in his tracks. Their eyes met and locked for a moment. Her pale blue eyes struck him like a punch in the chest. Then she continued past him. Shorter than the redhead behind him (Gio struggled to remember her name was Tiffany), this woman had blonde hair, a trim figure and walked with confidence.

Gio watched her go, feeling a tug, surprised to feel it come from his chest and not his loins.

Those eyes...

Tiffany, his hand in hers, pulled him toward the door. Giovanni glanced at her and the irritation on her face barely registered with him as they left the bar.

***

From his vantage point in the corner of the bar, Karl Winter watched Gio leave with the redhead, while at the same time ogling the blonde. Winter shook his head. Seated with his back to the door, Ridgeway hadn't noticed.

"What?" Ridgeway asked, turning to look.

"Gio just left with the redhead," Winter told him, glad he hadn't taken Ridgeway's bet earlier. "On the way out, he was eye-fucking the blonde over there."

Ridgeway looked at the blonde, nodding with approval. "Good taste," he said, then turned to face Winter. "Poor boy thinks too much with his little head instead of his big one."

"A wine glass and a woman's ass," Winter quoted the maxim that every policeman had been told since time immemorial. Those were the two things that would get a cop into more trouble than anything else. He wondered if they told the women officers something similar. Or if they had to.

Winter noticed Sgt. David Poole seated at the end of the bar. He considered inviting the sergeant to join them, but the way Poole hunched over his drink and the sour look on his face told Winter he didn't want the company. Besides, Ridgeway seemed particularly gloomy tonight and one dark mood at the table was enough for Winter.

Ridgeway drained the bottle of Budweiser. "You want a shot?" he asked Winter.

Winter shook his head.

Ridgeway shrugged. "Forget it, then. Can't drink that shit alone."

Winter sipped his beer, his second. Ridgeway waved to Rachel, the waitress, for his fourth. After patiently waiting for almost two hours, Winter sensed that Ridgeway was about to crack.

Ridgeway paid Rachel and sipped the beer. His eyes avoided Winter's. "Alice is having an affair," he said, head down, looking at the table. "She wants a divorce."

Winter pressed his lips together and sighed. Ridgeway's first marriage had ended in divorce after eleven years when they both realized they hated each other. Vindictive as hell, his first wife, Cynthia, took him to the cleaners. Ridgeway was still bitter over it. Two years passed before he met Alice and things softened up. Now he and Alice had four years together. Winter guessed the problems had begun about a year ago when Alice, fourteen years younger than Ridgeway, stopped coming to platoon functions.

"She's having an affair with a goddamn *fireman*," Ridgeway told him. "Can you believe that? It's not enough that I have to hear at work how everyone loves those pansies. Now one of them is banging my wife." His voice sank lower but became more angry and intense.

Winter didn't reply. His brother-in-law, Aaron, was a fireman in Portland, Oregon. He tried to think of something to say and failed. He took a long drink of beer instead.

Ridgeway shook his head, continuing to stare at his bottle. "I try to hate her, Karl. You know? Just hate her like I did Cynthia. But I can't. I love her. If she asked me to take her back, I would, even after all this."

"All of what?" Winter asked, feeling like he needed to say something.

Ridgeway motioned with his hands. "All of this. The sneaking around. The lying. The not calling." He paused. "The leaving."

Winter cocked an eyebrow. Ridgeway looked up and saw his expression. "Yeah," he admitted. "She moved out a month ago. She is living with the sonofabitch."

Jesus. Mark Ridgeway can keep a secret.

Winter excused himself to use the restroom and gave Mary a quick call, telling her the situation. She understood, like he knew she would. They exchanged "I love yous" and he hung up. Her voice comforted like a blanket. He wrapped it around himself as he joined Ridgeway to hear more about his lost love.

***

"Easy, Goddammit, *easy!*" James Mace pushed Andrea away as she snatched at the small piece of saran wrap in his hand. "You'll get yours, bitch. Now sit down and stop grabbing at me."

Andrea sat obediently on the edge of the dirty couch and rocked slightly. Forward and back, forward and back. She wrung her hands and stared at him.

Mace shook his head in disgust. "Where's Leslie?"

"I dunno."

"What do you mean, you don't know? Where'd she go?"

"I don't know," Andrea whined. "After you guys came back from the rip, you left again and then she left. She said you didn't get much cash. Maybe she went out on East Sprague to work a couple of dates or something."

"I got plenty of fucking cash!" Mace yelled. He waved the wrapped heroin in front of her. "I got this, didn't I?"

Andrea hugged herself, rubbing her arms. "Yeah, baby, you did. You are A-Number-One."

Mace grinned at her. He'd taught her that, how to talk the way the prostitutes in the Philippines did. She only used it when she wanted something, though.

"You shoulda seen it, An. Some doofy-looking guy in his forties was behind the counter. When I stuck that gun in his face, he started to cry!" Mace let out a bellowing laugh. "Fucking cried like a baby!"

Andrea grinned weakly and continued to hug herself and rock.

"You know," Mace said, "I shoulda put a bullet right through his nose. Blown his fucking face all over the wall!"

He trembled, but not from his desire for a fix. He felt alive. He felt powerful. Like a Ranger again.

He should have thought of all this a long time ago.

"Baby..." Andrea pleaded. "I'm hurtin'."

Mace looked at her. "Yeah. All right. Bring me your spoon."

Andrea scurried into the bedroom. Mace strode to the kitchen counter and pushed aside a pile of dirty plates. They clattered into the partially filled sink. He laid the drugs on the table, took his own works from the cupboard and removed his cooking spoon. He sensed Andrea at his side as he sliced off a thin piece of the brown, tarry substance.

"Here you go, baby," he whispered. "Here you go, you fucking bitch."

Andrea didn't even notice his epithet. She stood, transfixed on the knife as Mace slowly brought it over and scraped the tar onto her spoon. She hurried to the bedroom where she kept the rest of her kit.

Mace put the remaining chunk onto his spoon. He thought briefly of Leslie out on the streets of East Sprague, looking to whore her way to enough cash to score. Well, forget her, then. More for him and Andrea.

Mace stared at the heroin. *Sweet Brown. First I get to be a Ranger again and now I get the Sweet Brown.*

*God*damn, *life was good.*

Tuesday, August 20th
Graveyard Shift

Chisolm cruised slowly along residential streets with his windows open, letting the breeze flow through the police car. The smell of maple trees, freshly cut grass and occasionally the remains of an earlier barbecue wafted through the window.

A week had passed since his dismissal from the FTO program. The event still bothered him and he couldn't let it go. He was a good trainer. Hart, on the other hand, was a climber and a weasel. The man had no clue what made a good police officer. Now Payne, who should be looking for a job at the mall, worked with Bates, who Chisolm didn't think highly of, either. An okay officer, but way too easy on recruits. The chances of Payne getting fired while assigned to Bates were almost non-existent, a fact that Hart would have been aware of when he made the assignment.

Chisolm shook his head ruefully. Police officers in this town were asked to do a hard job. It required a compassionate soldier, something Chisolm tried to teach. However, the brass gave guidelines that required something of a cross between a counselor and a customer service representative at a department store. Citizens appreciated being treated that way, but criminals laughed at it.

Suck it up and drive on, you old soldier. No good pissing and moaning.

Chisolm turned onto Division Street and headed north. Aptly named Division, this center north-south street divided Adam Sector from Baker Sector. Chisolm continued north, turning west on Cleveland and dropping down to Corbin Park. A moment later, he realized that he was heading toward Sylvia's old house.

"Baker-123, a traffic stop." Stefan Kopriva called over the radio.

"Go ahead, -123."

"Eight eight one, Frank George Adam is the plate. We'll be at Perry and Fairview."

Chisolm liked Kopriva, one of the few younger officers who didn't buy into the line the brass was handing out. He rode with Chisolm for about a week during his training phase when his regular FTO had been sick. Kopriva learned his lessons well. Work hard, work safe, don't talk to the brass, and get the job done.

"Baker-123, start me backup!" Kopriva's sounded calm but Chisolm heard tension in the timbre his voice and the speed of his speech.

Chisolm whipped his car around and shot back to Division without bothering to call radio. He heard Janice dispatching Baker units. They copied but didn't broadcast their locations, leaving the air as open as possible for Kopriva.

Chisolm tore onto Division and buried his foot in the accelerator. Some officers requested back up even when they stopped Grandma, and they kept back up there until Grandma's name was cleared for warrants on the data channel. Other officers almost always went code four, such as Kopriva.

Especially Kopriva, who Chisolm knew had become somewhat of a code-four cowboy. If he asked for some quick back up, he wasn't kidding around.

Chisolm activated his overhead lights, clearing intersections with his siren. He sped up Foothills, a winding road that intersected with Perry about a block south of Fairview. He approached Perry and swung left, his tires squealing. No other units had checked out on scene yet.

"Adam-112, on scene at Perry," he told radio, rolling up next to Kopriva's patrol car. The driver's door stood wide open. Mid-way between the patrol car and a brown Chevy, Kopriva knelt on top of a black male sprawled on the ground. Kopriva held the suspect's hands clasped behind his neck. Two other black males sat in the car, one in the front seat, the other in the back. Kopriva leveled his gaze over the top of his gun at the suspect car. Each occupant held his hands high in the air.

"-112, advise on additional units."

Chisolm keyed his portable as he approached Kopriva, pointing his gun at the vehicle. "Keep them coming," he said simply. Then, to Kopriva, "Any outstanding?"

Kopriva shook his head. "No. Cover those two while I stuff this one."

Chisolm drew a bead on the one in the back seat, then searched the back of the car with his eyes. The trunk appeared secure. He wondered if any other subjects were lying down in the back seat.

Kopriva holstered his gun and frisked the suspect on the ground for weapons. "Hello, Isaiah. Remember me? Your little drive-by, looky-look the other night up in Hillyard? You had me real scared." Sarcasm dripped from his words. "By the way, you're under arrest." He lifted Morris to a seated position, then jerked him upright and led him back to the car.

Chisolm listened carefully, his eyes never leaving the Chevy. He knew Morris and it surprised him to see the gangster so quiet. Usually he had a lot to say. His nickname was "Cat," taken from the personality in the cat food commercials. Chisolm mused that aside from colorful spelling such as 'Lil Dawg or K-Illin', gang bangers tended to lack originality.

The rear-seat passenger turned to look back and Chisolm yelled, "Turn around!" The head snapped forward again.

The patrol car door slammed shut and Chisolm heard Kopriva return to his position. "Let's wait for one more car, Tom. Then we'll bring them out one at a time and cuff them. I've got nothing on those two yet, but I want them secure when I search the car."

Chisolm nodded. A prudent plan. There was a difference between being brash and weighing the risks.

Two more cars arrived. Kopriva advised radio code four with those units on scene. He relayed the plan to the other officers while Chisolm maintained his watch over the passengers.

In an authoritative voice, Kopriva barked orders at the passengers, while all officers moved to the position of cover offered by their cars. He brought the front seat passenger out first and directed him to walk backwards to a spot between the patrol vehicles. There, backup officers quickly and roughly cuffed him. They conducted a painstaking pat down for weapons but found none. After that, they secured him in a patrol car. The officers used the same procedure for the backseat passenger, again without incident.

Kopriva thanked the officers and asked them to stand by while he searched the car. Chisolm went forward with him. "What the hell happened?"

Kopriva opened the driver's door and laughed. "I recognized Morris in a car going the other way on Foothills. I knew he had a warrant, so I flipped around on him. As soon as I made the stop, Morris jumped out of the car and came running back at me."

Chisolm raised his eyebrows. "No kidding?"

"Nope." Kopriva leaned on the open door and spoke easily. "I could see his hands were empty, so I moved forward a few steps and waited for him. He was chattering about a mile a minute, threatening me and so forth. When I told him to get back in the car, he tried to push me."

"Tried?"

Kopriva grinned. "Morris is a sissy without a gun in his hand. I just parried his push, grabbed his wrist and foot-swept him. He went down hard. I think it knocked the wind out of him. After that, I just got control of him, drew down on his boys in the car and waited for the cavalry to arrive. Thanks for getting here so fast, Tom."

"Always," Chisolm said. "You want some help with the search?"

"Sure…" Kopriva said, distracted. He leaned into the car and removed something from beneath the driver's seat. It was a magazine, fully loaded.

Probably a .380, Chisolm figured.

"See if you can find the gun that goes with this," Kopriva said.

Chisolm and Kopriva tore the car apart, but found no gun. At Kopriva's direction, the other two officers pulled the suspects out of the patrol cars and searched them again. Still no gun.

Kopriva removed Morris from the back seat and searched him completely. In the process, he removed every item from the gangster's pockets and set them on the trunk of the patrol car.

"Man, you better get up off me," Morris told him.

"Shut up. Where's the gun?"

Morris smiled. "What gun, cracker?"

Kopriva ignored him and completed his search. Not finding any weapons on him, he sat Morris in the back of his patrol car again. Cliff Simms advised him that both of the other subjects were clear but had no driver's licenses. He tore off a notebook page with their information. Kopriva seemed surprised but thanked him.

"Damn," he whispered to Chisolm. "No gun, no crime."

"Is Morris a convicted felon? If he is, even having the ammo is illegal for him."

Kopriva frowned. "Not sure I can pin it on him. The mag was behind the seat. He was the driver."

"It's weak," Chisolm agreed. "Could they have thrown the gun out the window?"

Kopriva shook his head. "I never lost sight of them."

Chisolm shrugged. "Then all you have is the warrant and assault on an officer."

"Assault on an officer. That's still a traffic infraction, right?"

Chisolm chuckled. "It will be once the prosecutor is through with it."

"Oh, well." Kopriva sighed. "The Kitty Kat here is still going to jail. Let's cut his bonehead buddies loose."

Kopriva told the two black males they were not under arrest but were not driving away in that car, as neither had a valid driver's license. Chisolm watched as they transformed from meek to smug, rubbing their wrists were they'd been cuffed.

"What about him?" one asked.

"He's under arrest," Kopriva answered evenly.

"What for?"

"None of your business."

The gang banger snorted. "Shit, gee. He's under arrest for being black. That's all. That's all it ever is."

"I hear that," the second banger answered.

"Thank you," Kopriva said.

Both men eyed him strangely.

"What's that?" one asked.

"Thank you," Kopriva repeated. "I haven't been accused of racism yet tonight. Normally, it happens four or five times a night. I get edgy if I don't get in my quota. So thanks."

The bangers exchanged a glance.

"Can I count this as two, since you both seem to be accusing me?" Kopriva dead-panned. "Come on, man, I need the stats."

"Homes is crazy, man. Let's get outta here." Both men walked north on Perry, muttering to each other about racist cops.

"Nice work," Chisolm noted, as the two gangsters walked away.

"Thanks."

"See ya on the next one," Chisolm said and returned to his car. He noticed Cliff Simms locking the doors to the Chevy as he pulled away and headed back into Adam Sector.

**

Stefan Kopriva searched for a country station, knowing full well that Morris reviled cowboy tunes. He turned it up and faded it to the rear.

"Baker-123, I'll be en route to jail with a male for warrants. Mileage reset," he said into the radio mike and punched the reset button on the odometer.

"Baker-123, copy."

Morris seemed about to have a stroke in the back seat, jerking around and screaming. Kopriva let him be for a few more seconds. He loved trips to jail. No one in the patrol car but him and the bad guy. He could say whatever he wanted. It made up for all the times he had to hold his tongue.

He turned the radio down. "What's the problem, Kitty-kat?"

"Hey, man, fuck you. Fuck you!"

"Awww, what's the matter, Isaiah? Did that hurt? You did hit the pavement awful hard. Doesn't feel too good to get your ass kicked by a little white boy, does it?" Kopriva allowed himself to gloat.

Morris cursed at him some more. Looking in the rear-view mirror, Kopriva saw a small raspberry on Morris's cheek where he'd been held down against the pavement. Oh, well. Department policy stated that when an officer used the prone cuffing technique, a minor abrasion like that might occur. The policy, and the Chief himself, said that was just too bad for the arrestee.

"You got the wind knocked out of you, huh, Morris? And an ow-ie on your cheek. That kinda sucks."

"Kiss my ass, you white-boy, mother—"

Kopriva turned up the radio and sang along with Travis Tritt. He wished the song had been *Here's a Quarter, Call Someone Who Cares,* but all it took was country music of any kind to fuzz Morris up some more.

About a block from jail, he turned the radio down again.

"What, sir?" he asked in mock politeness.

"I said I want a picture of this."

"What?"

"This. On my face."

"Your boo-boo?"

"Fuck you, motherfucker. That's police brutality and I want a picture of it."

Kopriva paused as if considering the request. Then, "How about a picture of my foot up your ass?"

"Fuck you, faggot! I wanna talk to a supervisor."

Spittle flew from Morris' lips and struck the plastic shield. "I wanna see one of them gold-badge motherfuckers!"

"Call him from jail, kitty-kat."

"YOU CALL HIM!" Morris yelled, enraged.

Kopriva snorted. "I'm not a rookie, Cat-man. Save your act and call him your little old self." Ignoring Morris's tirade, he turned the radio back up and caught the tail end of the song as he pulled into jail.

***

Isaiah Morris struggled to get himself under control.

That fucking punk cop! Little wise-ass cracker! He thought he was so tough with a badge and a gun. Pulling his little tricky kung fu stunt on him back there at the car.

As the car slid into the jail sally-port, he forced himself to calm down. The jailers knew him and they didn't like him. If he gave them any reason, the racist motherfuckers would beat the black right out of him. He sat as still as he could manage, waiting while the cop exited the car and locked his gun in the gun safe.

I'd like to try you now, motherfucker, he raged silently. *Take these cuffs off and see, bitch.*

The cop walked into the booking area and several moments later, three jailers came out and headed for the car. He remained calm. Cops were always telling the jailers how crazy he was, but unless they saw it for themselves, they treated him mellow enough.

The first jailer, a fat one with a receding hairline, opened the door. "Are you going to cooperate tonight, Morris? Or do you want to go with the holding cell for a few hours?"

"I'm chillin'." Morris tried to keep his voice calm. "Just don't beat me like that last cop did. That man is a racist."

The door opened and pudgy hands helped him from the car. He walked into the officers booking area and straight through to the prisoner's receiving area. The fat jailer began booking him into jail, a process familiar enough to Morris. He cooperated completely, anticipating the jailer's questions and orders. He knew hard time and he knew easy time. There was a lot less lee-way in here than out in the street. And fewer witnesses.

The hot-shot cop who arrested him came in and read him his warrant. He knew it was required by law and made no effort to interrupt.

"This is your warrant," he intoned. "It's in Superior Court for failure to appear on an original charge of possession of crack cocaine. Bail is set at $25,000. Signed on August 24th of this year by Judge Antonio Calabrese." The cop looked up. "Any questions?"

"Fuck you," whispered Morris.

"Same to you," the cop replied in a low, even voice and turned to walk away.

"I'll get you," Morris gritted, anger seething inside him. "One-eighty-seven, motherfucker." The California penal code for homicide, 'one-eighty seven' was a common way among gang members to threaten to kill someone.

The cop must have known what it meant because he snarled something under his breath and took a step toward Morris. Two jailers intervened, holding the young hothead back. Morris wished the jailers hadn't been there so the cop could have hit him. How nice it'd be to press charges against him with all these witnesses who were too stupid to lie!

The jailers walked the cop out of the receiving area. Morris smiled and blew him a kiss. "One-eighty-seven," he repeated as the cop reached the door.

"Shut up, Isaiah," the fat jailer told him, "or we will do this the hard way."

Morris remained quiet. He answered all questions and signed that his property had been removed. Then he signed his booking notification on the warrant with $25,000 bail and for assaulting an officer with $5000 bail. He cooperated patiently as the jailer meticulously snapped his picture and fingerprinted him. Finally, they allowed him to use the phone.

It took one phone call to his cuz, $4500 out of his stash and a second call, this to a bail bondsman, before he was booked back out. The process going out seemed even quicker than going in, an irony that was not lost on Morris. He hit the street and got into T-Dog's car exactly one hour and forty-eight minutes after being brought to jail.

**

Stefan Kopriva left the property room where he'd just written his report and placed the magazine and ammunition on the property book. He heard a screech of tires from the corner. A Cadillac approached, the silhouette of a head sticking out the rear window.

Kopriva drew his pistol and held it at his side. He moved quickly to the patrol car for cover.

The car rolled closer and he saw Morris in the window.

"One-eighty-seven, motherfucker-r-r-r-r-r!" the gangster yelled.

Kopriva raised his gun in case Morris fired, but the tires squealed and the Cadillac pulled away. At the intersection, they took a right and disappeared.

What is he doing out of jail already? Kopriva shook his head. *What a screwed up system.*

When he holstered his gun, he suddenly realized he was breathing rapidly. *Damned adrenaline.* Kopriva took several deep breaths, taking his time and forcing himself calm before he got into the patrol car and started the engine. By the time he notified dispatch that he was clear, he felt steady again.

Wednesday, August 21st
Day Shift

There are some things that a man should be left alone while doing. As far as Sgt. David Poole was concerned, working on his car was one of them.

He adjusted the valves on his 1969 Chevrolet Chevelle Super Sport. It had a huge engine, a 396 large-block that sucked gas like a greedy bitch. He'd put a stock, stiff four-speed in it and it had never given him any trouble. Then again, he never missed a power-shift, either.

He'd sipped a Michelob throughout the valve adjustment and now that they were fine-tuned, he allowed himself a deep draught. Then his sister Angela arrived and broke into the sanctity of his garage.

"Davey?"

Damn, he hated being called that.

"Over here, Ang."

Angela Poole-Nyerson appeared at the edge of the garage. "Working on the racecar?" she teased.

"Yup." Poole took another slug of his Michelob.

"I've been trying to reach you all day. Have you been home?"

"Been home." Poole started to wipe off his tools and put them away. *Damn. And today had been a fairly decent day, too. Not like I get many of those these days.* "I turned off the phone."

"Hiding from work again?" she needled.

He looked up. "Would you want the Bon Marché calling you on your days off?"

Angela smiled and winked. "What days off?"

Poole softened the tone in his voice. He knew Angela meant well. Hell, she was the only one in the family who even talked to him. He probably shouldn't alienate her as well, but he had no patience any more. That thought ran through his mind like a logic problem, and he found that he really didn't care either way.

"What did you want, Angela?" He wiped off a wrench, and hung it on his pegboard.

"Okay, grump. Mom's birthday is next Monday. Donald and I are putting together a surprise party for her, a picnic at Franklin Park. Can you come?"

Why was she asking? Poole wondered.

"I don't know," he said.

"Come on, Davey. It's her birthday."

"No one will miss me if I'm not there," he told her.

"Well, what do you expect?" Angela flared.

"Nothing." He refused to look at her but his jaw clenched. "I expect nothing."

Angela swore and turned away. Then she stopped.

"No. You need to be told." She stepped around the car to face Poole. "I really want to know what you expect. You cut yourself off from everyone in the family. Your kids never see you, your parents, your ex-wife, not me or Donny. What are we supposed to do?"

Poole didn't answer, so she went on.

"I'm sorry your life is the pits, Davey. I'm sorry you got divorced, that you've been alone this past year. I'm sorry if your career isn't going the way you want. But all I'm asking you to do is show up for one lousy afternoon on your own mother's birthday." Angela paused. She opened her mouth to say more, but stopped again, half-sobbing instead. "Goddamn you."

Poole looked up and caught her eye. Tears streamed down her face, but it didn't move him. Through clenched teeth, he told her, "Don't preach to me, sis. Everyone in this whole happy family knew Sherrie was fooling around on me. Did anyone think to tell me? No."

"It was none of our business!" she protested, wiping her eyes.

"Well, it certainly became everyone's business when I filed for divorce, didn't it? When, suddenly, I became the bad guy?"

"No one can talk to you!" Angela yelled at him and ran out of the garage.

Poole listened to her descending footfalls. He heard her Jeep start and squeal off. He tried to care but failed.

It wasn't so bad that he got the divorce. It was

being played the fool that made him angry. He never really loved Sherrie. Just a pair of kids themselves, they'd married because she'd gotten pregnant. It wasn't like she'd been the love of his life, but somehow being duped and having everyone know it seemed worse when no heartbreak had been involved. Or maybe he just noticed the anger more because there wasn't any heartbreak taking up space on his emotional hard drive.

Poole replaced the valve gasket and cover, trying not to hurry. Anger continued to build inside of him. Anger at his family, whom he considered a pack full of traitors, at Sherrie, for not just breaking it off with him first before she started sleeping around, and the job. The fucking job. Hart making lieutenant and everyone considering him the el-tee's flunkie. Hart probably most of all. Some friend.

Life just plain sucks. I need some heavy metal.

He pushed a button and Metallica roared out of his boom box. Carefully, he tightened down the valve cover. By the time he slammed the hood, he really needed to drive.

***

The alarm tone caught Karl Winter by surprise. Scarface had never hit before eighteen hundred, and Winter couldn't recall a robbery on day shift since June or so. He slipped his sandwich back into his cooler and brushed the crumbs off his shirt as he listened intently.

"Suspect fled eastbound. White male, tall and thin

wearing black jeans and a blue windbreaker. Long black hair with a scar on the left side of his face."

Winter dropped the car into gear and headed in the direction of the robbery. He decided to put his theory to the test, so he drove to Grand Boulevard and parked. He watched cars as they cruised past, looking for single females driving large cars.

Ridgeway and Giovanni both radioed their arrival at the area of the robbery near Southeast Blvd.

There!

Winter saw a slender white female with dark, stringy hair westbound on 29th approaching Grand. She appeared nervous. A thrill shot through Winter. That could be it.

He radioed in his intention to stop the vehicle. The dispatcher sent the south side corporal, Jim McGee, to back him up. Winter swung in behind the large car and waited for her to clear the intersection and continue for another two blocks. As he watched, the driver nervously glanced in her rear-view mirror. When she changed lanes without signaling, he turned on his overheads and broadcasted his final location.

"Paul-314, I'm about a minute off," McGee advised.

Winter approached the vehicle carefully. He rested his hand lightly on his gun, something he rarely did any more. The driver watched him, stock-still. Both of her hands clutched the steering wheel.

Winter scanned the back seat. Empty. And

unusually clean. Nothing other than three unopened cans of motor oil lay on the vacuumed floor. The front passenger seat was likewise empty.

"Is there a problem, officer?"

Winter met her gaze. He saw nothing there beyond the nervousness most motorists displayed when stopped by the police. "You failed to signal for a lane change."

The woman turned red. "Oh, my God, did I?"

Winter nodded.

"I'm so sorry," she said.

Winter asked for her license and she handed it over. Winter scrutinized it, his suspicion fading.

"Charlie-253, I've got him by the Buck Bonanza." Ridgeway's voice held steady. *"He's heading toward a blue Datsun pickup."*

"-257, I'm with him."

"Paul-314, I can divert if -251 is code four."

Winter keyed his mike as he handed the woman back her license. "-251 is clear and en route."

The Buck Bonanza, where everything in the store cost just one dollar, was located at about 27th and Freya, a straight shot down 29th. Winter, usually a cautious driver, activated his lights and siren and drove like a graveyard officer. Civilian cars peeled off to the right to make way for him. He cranked the volume on his police radio and listened, knowing it would all be over before he could get there.

As he approached Southeast Boulevard, Gio's voice came over the air, out of breath. *"Charlie-257, one in custody. Have units lower their code."*

Winter shut off his sirens but kept his lights on, as he cruised into the parking lot. He spotted Ridgeway rummaging through a small blue pickup. Gio stood over a prone and handcuffed white male. Winter parked his car and approached.

Gio smiled at him and held up a black wig. "Lookee here, Karl."

Winter returned the grin.

Gio hooted. "Whew! Day tour nabs Scarface! Graveyard would've needed forty troops and an hour to do this."

Winter eyed the suspect lying very still on the ground. Hands cuffed behind his back, the man's head faced toward Winter. He remained motionless, his eyes wide open and staring. Winter would have suspected the man was dead if hadn't noticed him breathing heavily and blinking occasionally.

Karl Winter frowned. He saw a fake scar on the left side of the suspect's face. It hung limply from his cheek, partially peeled away. Winter also noticed a gash on the man's brow. A trickle of blood flowed from it.

"Stupid," Winter muttered.

Ridgeway joined them. A black gun dangled by his pen in the trigger-guard. Winter noticed it sway back and forth easily as Ridgeway approached. Too easily.

"Plastic," Ridgeway told them both. "Moron robbed the store with a toy gun."

Gio shook his head. He handed the wig to Ridgeway who put it in an evidence bag, along with the plastic gun. Then Gio and Winter stood the suspect up and put him in Gio's car. "I'll take him to Major Crimes if you want to stay with the scene, Mark."

Ridgeway nodded as Corporal McGee pulled up. With Poole on his day off, McGee was in command of the platoon. *Not that these veterans needed much commanding,* Winter thought.

After all, he added with a smile, *they'd caught the infamous Scarface robber.*

And that was something Swing shift *and* Graves had failed to do after fourteen chances.

***

When the phone call from Dispatch came, Lt. Alan Hart had been interviewing a citizen who wanted to file a complaint against one of his officers. Officer Jack Stone, a ten-year-veteran, worked the north side. Based on what the citizen had told him thus far, it sounded like a founded demeanor complaint to Hart.

Now, he hung up the phone with mixed feelings. It was a feather in his cap that Scarface had been caught by his shift, and not Saylor's. But it precluded any need for his task force, which the patrol captain had tentatively approved. As a result, he attained some small glory where he could have achieved a lot.

I just have to make the best of it.

He turned his attention back to the citizen. "Mr. Weston, I appreciate you coming in. You have a valid complaint. I will definitely forward this information to our Internal Affairs Unit. Someone will contact you for another interview. If it's not convenient to come in, they can conduct it by telephone."

Mr. Weston rose and shook Hart's hand. "Thank you. I hope the officer doesn't get in too much trouble. I just wanted to let you know what had happened."

Hart gave his most political smile. "It's citizens like you who help us make this a better department."

Mr. Weston left, obviously pleased with himself.

Hart locked his office and hustled over to Major Crimes to check on the Scarface investigation.

***

Duke's, the bar preferred by patrol, pulsed with excitement. Still flush with their success, Gio and Ridgeway celebrated. They stood at the bar, re-telling the story over and over to cops and patrons alike. Johnny, the bartender, and Rachel, the waitress, had each heard the tale at least six times.

In high spirits, Gio tipped back his beer. He found the day tour comfortable. They handled a lot of boring calls, but you couldn't beat the hours. During the summer, all the little hotties came out in shorts and tank tops, providing nice scenery, too. Even so, he often longed for more action. Today had satisfied that longing.

"There I was," Ridgeway told Jack Stone, the newest arrival, "on routine patrol."

Stone smiled at the age-old joke. "Don't you mean, 'It was a dark and stormy night' or something like that?"

"This is a police story," Ridgeway told him. Though not yet five o'clock, both men had downed two beers and two shots. Gio consciously slowed down after the first triumphant beer and shot. "Anyway, so I see this guy sneaking around the parking lot—"

"Sneaking? In broad daylight?"

"Yes, like the idiot that he is." Ridgeway paused to take a slug from his beer. "Anyway, I know it's him. He's got a paper bag hanging out of his jacket pocket and long black hair. It's obviously a wig. I mean, you can see that from clear across the parking lot."

"What's he wearing a jacket for, anyway?" Stone added. "It's almost sixty degrees out today."

Ridgeway stared at Stone in mock-anger. "You want to tell this story?"

"No, go ahead." Stone grinned.

"All right. So I go buzzing up there as he gets into the pickup. I see Gio coming the other way. We jump out and run up to the truck. I've got my piece out – "

"So do I," Gio chimed in.

"– and I'm telling this maggot to show me his hands. Gio's got a bead on him through the passenger window, and I'm about a step behind the door." He took another drink.

Gio noticed the door open and a woman enter the bar. Immediately, he felt a stab of butterflies in his stomach. It was *her*, the blonde from the other night, the one with the pale blue eyes. She glided in and took a seat in the far corner. He noted with some satisfaction that she was alone.

Gio's mouth went suddenly dry. He took a sip of his beer and rubbed his palms on his jeans.

Ridgeway set his glass down and continued his story. "Moron has his hands on the wheel, but now he's getting confused. I don't see a gun, but the paper bag has fallen out of his jacket. Money is all over the front seat. He doesn't know what to do, and he's not listening to me. I've got his door swung open. I'm telling him to get out of the truck. Then he starts reaching inside his jacket."

Stone shook his head, disbelieving. "Stupid bastard. Why didn't you shoot him?"

Ridgeway shrugged. "Coulda."

"But…"

"I cracked him upside the head instead."

Stone chuckled. "With what? Your gun?"

Ridgeway nodded.

Stone laughed out loud.

"Tore that fake scar right off his face. It was hanging off his cheek." Ridgeway allowed himself a rare grin. "Hanging right below the new *real* scar I gave him."

"That is great," Stone chuckled. "Mr. Master Shooter turns Wyatt Earp. Priceless."

Stone clapped Ridgeway on the shoulder. "You saved that guy's life, Mark. You're a bona fide hero. He should be dead. But now that you saved his life, he'll probably file a complaint and sue the city."

Ridgeway's grin melted. "Probably. Who cares?"

Stone shrugged. "Speaking of which, that goddamn Lieutenant Hart called me in today. I got another IA complaint. Completely unfounded."

Ridgeway snorted. "Big surprise."

The two men paused to take a long draft of beer.

Gio waved Johnny over. The bartender leaned forward toward Gio. "Yeah?"

Gio motioned to the blonde. He didn't even have to tell the bartender what he wanted to know. Good thing, too, because his throat and mouth were dry again.

Johnny studied her for a moment. Gio could see the computer hard drive behind the bartender's eyes as it ground through information. *Accessing, accessing.* Then he turned back to Gio.

"Marilyn. That's her name." He kept wiping the bar in front of Gio. "She comes in once in a while, sometimes alone, sometimes she meets a few girlfriends. I think she works near here. Not a groupie, though, Gio."

Gio nodded his thanks. Without another word, Johnny left to serve another customer.

Stone recounted his meeting with Hart. "I mean, the guy will take something, *anything,* and blow it up so he can spend twenty minutes lecturing you. What a prick."

Ridgeway nodded. "What was the complaint for?"

"Some old buzzard I told to move along at that fatal accident we had at Illinois and Perry last week."

"That one where the high school girl died?"

"Yeah. Her little Toyota Corolla was t-boned by a 4x4. Anyway, people were acting like it was an interactive version of *COPS* or something, and I was getting tired of moving them along. This guy musta tried to look or something. I don't even remember him."

"Hart." Ridgeway grunted the word like it was a curse and then threw back another slug of his Budweiser. "You hear he fired Chisolm from the FTO program?"

Stone nodded. "Yeah. I heard Chisolm got so torqued he pulled a gun on him in the office."

Ridgeway frowned. "C'mon, Jack. You really think Chisolm would pull a gun on the lieutenant?"

Stone stared back at him, blinked and said nothing.

"Okay," Ridgeway conceded, "but do you think he would still be working here if he did?"

"No. And I think Hart would be six feet under. The prick."

Johnny put another round of shots in front of them. Ridgeway raised his glass. "I'll drink to that. "

"Me, too."

"To hope," Ridgeway said sarcastically. Both sipped.

"Hey, guys!" came a familiar voice. Janice Koslowski, a forty-one year old radio dispatcher, walked up to the bar and put her arm around Ridgeway's shoulder. "My hero!" she said, planting a kiss on his cheek. Then, looking at Gio, she reached out and put her other arm around him. "You too, tall, dark and slutty."

Gio grinned, but glanced toward the blonde. She hadn't noticed him.

"What are you doing here?" Ridgeway asked her. "Shouldn't you be asleep?"

"Night off," Janice told him, pushing back her long brown hair and smiling. "I stopped in to pick up my paycheck and heard the news. Nice job, fellas."

Ridgeway took a sip from his shot glass. "Yeah, did they tell you we almost got killed?"

Janice looked upset. "What?!"

Ridgeway nodded. "Yeah. Rookie dispatcher completely screwed up on the call. Almost got us killed." He took another sip from his glass. "If only we had a veteran dispatcher..."

"Oh, nice!" Janice slapped his shoulder hard. "You had me going for a second."

Ridgeway chuckled. Gio raised his eyebrows in surprise. He hadn't seen him do that in a while.

Janice shook her head, smiling. "Well, I see one thing hasn't changed since I went to graveyard. Mark Ridgeway is still a mean s.o.b."

Ridgeway raised his near-empty shot glass. "At your service, ma'am. Have a drink with me?"

Janice grinned. "Mark, I don't know. With you, it is never just one."

"Can't have just one. It gets lonely in my stomach. Wants company. Gotta send it some of its brothers."

Janice's smile didn't fade. "Okay, mister. I'll have *one.*" She motioned to Johnny and pointed at Ridgeway's glass and gave Johnny one finger.

"It'll get loh-ohnllyyy..." Ridgeway crooned.

Jack Stone began to sing "One is the loneliest number..."

"Shut up and tell me what really happened," Janice chuckled.

Gio slipped from the stool and walked toward Marilyn. He heard Janice and Ridgeway pause briefly—probably to watch him go—then Janice asked Ridgeway for all the "dirty details."

Marilyn sat alone, sipping from a small glass. She noticed his approach about two steps away, her eyes inviting but cautious.

What do I say?

"Hello," she said, her voice friendly.

"Hello," Gio answered. "Can I, uh, sit with you for a few minutes?"

She paused, considering. Then, "Sure. I'm only planning to stay until I finish this drink, though."

Gio sat across from her. *God, she's beautiful.* He'd only gotten a brief look that first night and his experience taught that imagination generally fills in what you don't see. Imagination tends to be optimistic and reality often disappointing. Not in her case, though. She looked even lovelier than he remembered.

"What's your name?" she asked.

"Anthony. Giovanni. My friends call me Gio."

"I'm Marilyn."

"Nice to meet you."

Now what I am supposed to say?

Gio wiped his sweaty palms on the front of his jeans. He was afraid to use a line on her, afraid to bullshit with her like he did with all the bunnies that usually came in here. It hit him like a slap up the side of the head when he realized he had little to say without those lines.

There was an uncomfortable pause. They looked at each other and Gio thought he saw something in her eyes. *Does she feel this, too? Already? This... pull?*

The pause went on long enough to outlive its own discomfort and became an easy silence. Both sipped their drinks. Marilyn finally broke the silence.

"This is a good song."

Gio listened to the song drifting from the jukebox. He recognized Stevie Nicks' sultry voice.

"Very good song." He felt like an idiot. What was the name of the song? He'd heard it a million times, but he couldn't think of the title.

She smiled at his obvious nervousness, took another sip and finished her drink. Gio panicked. She had said she was leaving after that drink—

Marilyn dug in her purse, removed her wallet and dropped some money on the table. Then she looked up at Gio and smiled again.

"Listen," she said. "I have to go. I'm meeting a girlfriend."

Gio nodded glumly. He wanted to ask her out but knew he hadn't laid the groundwork, knew he would only stumble over his own tongue. *You blew it,* he told himself angrily.

Marilyn took a pen from her purse. She met Gio's gaze.

Those eyes!

"Maybe we could go out to lunch sometime?" She smiled.

He sat there, shocked. He took so long to answer that she dropped her gaze and started to put her pen away.

"Yes!" Gio answered too forcefully. She looked up. Gio softened his voice. "I mean, yes. Thank you. You just took me by surprise."

She seemed to accept that. "What's your phone number?" she asked. "I'll call you in a few days?"

"Okay." He gave her the number.

"See you" She slid out of the booth.

"Bye."

Marilyn gave him a smile and left. He followed her to the door with his eyes, watching her leave. It was only then that he realized how fast his heart was beating.

Kopriva left the roll call room and walked downstairs to the records desk on the main floor. With Scarface out of commission, it figured to be a slow night. Maybe he'd chase some warrants. Newly issued warrants were stacked by the counter for officers to look at until the records personnel found time to input them into the computer system. Kopriva thumbed through the pile.

"Hi, Stef," came a female voice from behind the counter.

Kopriva looked up to see Maria Soledad smiling at him. The thirty-year-old Puerto Rican woman had the longest and darkest hair Kopriva had ever seen. He smiled back.

"Hi, Maria. *Cómo Estás?*"

"Bien. Y tú?"

"Good," he replied, having reached the limit of his Spanish-speaking skills.

"Did you hear they caught that robber?"

Kopriva nodded, perusing the warrants. "Yeah. Can you believe it was a bunch of day-shifters that did it?"

"Well, they have more experience, don't they?"

"Yeah, I suppose, when they want to work. I think coffee is the highest priority for some of them."

"Oh, Stef, you're being mean. *Tú eres malo.*"

"Call 'em as I see 'em," Kopriva said. He pulled a felony drug warrant for a man named Martin Belzer from the stack and handed it to Maria. "Could you run him up for me?"

"Sure." Maria sat at her desk and quickly entered the name into the computer. It amazed Kopriva how fast she could type. She waited several minutes for the system to come back with a response.

"You type too fast for the computer, *Señora.*"

"Ten words per minute would be too fast for this system," Maria replied.

"Government spending at its best," Kopriva joked.

"*Es la verdad,*" she said absently. "Looks like you hit the jackpot on this one. In addition to this felony hit here, he has another felony warrant for drugs, plus three misdemeanor warrants."

"So five total?"

"No, actually seven," she answered, staring at the screen. "Here's two misdemeanor hits out of Seattle. And they're extraditable, too."

"Great. Can you print that off for me and confirm the local ones?"

Maria hit several keys and a printer began to buzz next to her computer. "You want a picture of Mr. Ten Most Wanted?"

"Maria, you are a dream."

"More like a nightmare," she chuckled, calling up a booking photo of Martin Belzer and printing it. She handed the printout and the black-and-white photo to Kopriva. "I'll check the file and be back in a few."

"Great. Thanks."

Kopriva looked at the printout. Belzer's listed address was 1814 N. Quincey, in Adam Sector. He should probably have an Adam Sector officer go with him. Maybe Chisolm—

"Hey, Stef, what's up?" Katie MacLeod appeared at his side and reached for the warrant stack. "You finished with these?"

"Yeah. I already found my gold mine." He waved the picture of Belzer.

"Really? How's that?"

"Mr. Belzer here has a butt-load of warrants."

"A *butt-load*? I see. Is that more or less than an ass-full?"

Kopriva considered. "I think it's the metric conversion."

Katie laughed. "Very funny. How many does he have?"

"Seven. Two of 'em are felony drug. His last known address is in Adam Sector. You want to come along?"

"Sure. I have to give Kevin a call first, though."

Kopriva made a whip-cracking sound.

"Shut-up. He said it was important."

"Okay, okay." Kopriva raised his hands in surrender. "I'll meet you at the elementary school there at Monroe and Maxwell."

"Okay. See you." Katie walked away.

Kopriva made the whip-crack noise again. Katie stuck her hand in the middle of her back and gave him the finger.

"Such an angry finger," Maria tut-tutted as she returned from the warrant confirmation. "What on earth did you say to her?"

Kopriva shrugged. "I dunno. Who knows with women? Right, Maria?"

"You better watch it, or I will give these warrants to someone else."

Kopriva bowed. "*Perdóneme.*"

"In that case, your warrants are confirmed. *Buena suerte.*"

Kopriva thanked her and left.

***

"Come on, Janice! One more!"

"No more, Mark. I gotta get going." Janice

Koslowski put her coat on. Gio and Stone had left an hour ago. They probably thought they were doing her a favor by leaving her alone with Ridgeway. They weren't. She'd heard about Ridgeway's wife and the fireman. There was no way she was getting involved with a cop. Not again, and not with one on the rebound.

"Come on! It's early yet."

"Early if you started at seven," Janice told him. "You've been here since four o'clock. It's ten now. It's time to go."

"Fine. Go."

"You should leave, too. I'll call you a cab."

"I'm fine. I'll drink coffee for awhile and drive home."

Janice shook her head. "There isn't enough coffee in Colombia to sober you up, Mark."

"I'm not taking a cab. It's degrading."

Janice resisted the urge to argue. It would just cause him to get more stubborn. "Okay. I'll drive you home."

Ridgeway glanced up. His drunken gaze penetrated her, and she felt a pang in her stomach. *Another time, another place.*

"People will talk," Ridgeway told her.

"A grizzled veteran police officer once told me how to respond to people talking like that."

136

"How?"

"I think he said, 'Screw 'em.' Or something equally eloquent."

Ridgeway grinned. "Yeah. Screw 'em. I like that. Who told you that?"

Janice chuckled. "Some idiot."

"Who?"

"You."

Ridgeway let out a hearty laugh. He finished his drink in a gulp. "All right, Jan. Let's go." He tossed a twenty on the bar and waved at Johnny, who waved back. Despite his seeming unconcern, Janice knew the bartender had been monitoring the situation.

Outside in the parking lot, the warm night air smelt of weak beer and auto fumes. Janice tried to hold Ridgeway by the arm to support him, but he found that degrading as well. He slipped his arm around her shoulders. That fulfilled the same purpose of allowing her to support him, so she didn't protest.

When they reached her Saturn coupe, she unlocked the passenger door and Ridgeway flopped onto the front seat. She swung his legs in with little help from him and shut the door. Then she went around to the driver's side, got in and started the car.

Ridgeway sat silently as they drove, his eyes fixed straight ahead. Then he turned slowly to Janice and asked, "Is this a little Jap car?"

"No."

"Because if this was made by those little market-greedy zipper-heads, you can just let me out right now. Little yellow bastards. Shot up my Dad in World War II, killed my brother in 'Nam. Tried to shoot me in 'Nam, but couldn't do it. Then you know what they did?" He slapped the dashboard. "The little sonsabitches came over here and bought the auto plant my Dad worked at and laid him off. Maybe they were pissed about not killing him in the war and thought they'd come over here and finish the job."

"Mark—"

"Worked, too. He died six months after he got laid off."

"Mark, it's a Saturn. It's not Japanese. It's made in the USA. And there's a difference between Japanese and Vietnamese. They're two completely different—"

"Made in the USA? No kidding?"

"Yes. Mark, you know all this. I know you know cars."

Ridgeway shrugged. "It's not the same as it used to be. They all look alike. There's a thousand makes and models now. Nothing is the same as it used to be. Nothing."

Janice didn't answer. She continued to drive.

Ridgeway was quiet a long while, then asked her, "Really now, this is made in the USA?"

138

Janice nodded. "Made in Tennessee."

"No kidding. You're my kind of girl, Janice. Do you have a gun at home?"

"Of course."

"What kind?"

"A .357 magnum. Why?"

"Just wondering. You are just about the perfect woman, Janice. Are you an NRA member?" Ridgeway's words slurred noticeably.

"No. Every two years I vote for the person I think will do the best job. Otherwise, I try to stay out of anything political."

"Well, everyone has a flaw," Ridgeway mused. "But damn near the perfect woman. I should have married you, Janice."

"You're drunker than a skunk."

"Maybe so, but I still should have married you."

Janice drove the rest of the way to Ridgeway's house without saying another word. She didn't want to remind him that the chance had been there sixteen years ago or that she hadn't seemed so perfect to him then.

Ridgeway's house stood in the middle of the 5000 block of North Wren. Typical two-bedroom, middle class rancher, perfect for a couple with no kids. Janice pulled up in front and shut off her lights. She looked at Ridgeway, who dozed in the passenger's seat.

Somehow, Janice got him awake and walked him clumsily to the front door. She found his keys in his jacket pocket and let them inside. Ridgeway staggered through the door and flopped onto the couch.

The house struck her as surprisingly well-kept for a house with a single male living in it. The dishes were done in the kitchen. She filled a glass with tap water, then went into the bathroom. Except for a towel on the floor in the corner, it, too, was clean. She found aspirin in the medicine chest above the sink and returned to the living room.

Ridgeway hadn't moved. She nudged him.

"Here, take these aspirin."

"Hmmmmmm?"

"C'mon, Mark. You're gonna feel like hell in the morning as it is. Take the aspirin."

"Mmmmmm." Mark sat up squinting. With her help, he took the three tablets and a swallow of water. Then he flopped back onto the couch.

Janice removed his shoes and lifted his feet off of the floor and onto the cushions. In the hall closet she found a quilt. Back in the living room, she covered him with it.

"Goodnight, my little robber-catcher." She kissed him lightly above his eyebrow.

"'Night, Alice," Ridgeway murmured.

Janice tried not to be hurt, but failed. Without being gentle, she tucked the quilt around him, dropped his keys on the small table by the door and locked it behind her.

She drove toward home. *Stupid. I'm so stupid.* She turned on the car radio and tried not to think.

***

Kopriva waited in the parking lot of the elementary school, surprised at how late Katie was. He'd checked with radio to see if she was in service yet and she wasn't. That phone call must have been a long one.

Eventually, a police car pulled into the dark lot and glided up next to him. Katie lowered her window. "Sorry I took so long."

Kopriva thought she sounded a little strange, like she had been crying. "Are you okay?"

"I'm fine. Where's this guy live?"

Kopriva turned on his interior light and read her the address aloud.

"Okay. Meet you there," she said and drove off.

Something was definitely wrong, Kopriva knew. He also knew that if Katie didn't want to tell him, she wasn't going to. She had a stubborn streak that way.

Kopriva drove quickly to the address, parked up the street and walked in. Katie met him behind a tree in front of a house painted white with a well-tended yard. Kopriva frowned. He doubted Belzer still lived there. Druggers seldom showed much concern about the house or yard where they lived. Besides, they generally didn't stay in any one place for long.

After peering through the window and finding the inside just as tidy as the yard, Kopriva rang the door-bell. A red-headed woman in her early twenties opened the door'.

"Hello?" She said, and then noticed their uniforms. "Is something wrong?"

"No, ma'am," Kopriva assured her. "Can we come in and talk with you for a moment?"

"Um, yeah, I guess." She stepped aside and allowed them to enter.

Once inside, Kopriva asked her name.

"Michelle Belzer," she answered. "Why?"

"We're looking for Martin Belzer. Is he your husband...?"

Michelle snorted. "Hell, no! Unfortunately, he's my uncle. What'd he do?"

"We just need to talk to him," Kopriva said. "Does he live here?"

"No," Michelle answered. "He did for awhile, but my parents kicked him out. He's pretty well burned his bridges with most of the family. He does drugs, if you didn't know."

"How long ago was he living here?"

Michelle considered. "A month or so. His mail still comes here, though."

"Any idea where he might be now?"

"Not really. That's why I still have a ton of his mail. His Mom and his sister still support him somewhat. Either one of them might know."

"Who would be more likely to help us find him?"

"My Aunt, his sister. Depending on how she feels about him at the moment."

"All right. Do you mind if we check around here really quick? That way we can tell our boss that he's definitely not here."

She shrugged. "Sure."

While Kopriva checked, Katie stayed with Michelle. Kopriva overheard Michelle asking Katie numerous questions about being a female cop. Katie answered her politely, but seemed a little short, which was unlike her.

Kopriva's search of the house turned up no sign of Belzer and no evidence of a male living at the house. That completed, Kopriva asked Michelle for the number and address of Belzer's mother and sister. She read them to him from her address book. Kopriva wrote them in his notebook and thanked her.

"Anytime," Michelle said. "That jerk stole eight hundred dollars of my tuition money one quarter last year from my parent's house. I hope he rots in hell."

Revenge. "I'll see what I can do," Kopriva said "You'll have to settle for jail, though. I'm not in charge of hell. Yet."

Michelle laughed at his joke as he and Katie left.

Back in his car, Kopriva plugged in his cellular phone. He'd bought it for use on the job when it became apparent the department could never afford to supply officers with one. It had proven to be a valuable tool.

Katie pulled her car next to him. "So?"

"So now I call mom and sister and see if they will give me a lead."

Kopriva dialed the sister's number. The line was busy.

"Busy," he told Katie. "You think Michelle is in there ratting us off?"

Katie shrugged.

Kopriva dialed the mother's number. The phone rang twice, then a male voice answered. "Hello?"

"Hello? Is Mrs. Belzer home?"

"No. This is her son. Can I help you?"

Kopriva smiled in surprise. "Martin Belzer?"

"Yeah. Who's this?"

Damn! His smile faded, but he thought quickly. "It's the United States Postal Service, Mr. Belzer."

"Who?"

"The Post Office, sir. Actually, Mr. Belzer, we were hoping to locate you. My name is James Zurn. I work in misdirected mail and forwarding addresses. I understand you used to live at—" Kopriva paused, pretending to shuffle through some papers. "At 1814 N. Quincey. Is that correct?"

"Yes."

"Well, sir, we've been getting mail back from that address stating that you are no longer there. However, we show a last name of Belzer still residing there."

"Yeah. My brother lives there. I moved out a while back."

"I see. Okay, well, if you can give me an updated address, I'll enter it into the computer right now and you should start getting all your mail again."

"I'm living with my mother right now," he said and gave the address.

Kopriva had him repeat part of it several times and complained, "This computer is slow sometimes."

In the car next to him, Katie chuckled. "You're pushing your luck," she whispered.

"Maybe that's why the mail takes so long," Belzer joked.

"Actually, sir, if you compare the US Postal system with other western nations in Europe, we are fourteen to seventeen percent faster on average. Only Japan and Denmark have a faster mail system."

"Oh." Belzer was quiet for a moment. Then he said, "Isn't it kind of late to be doing this kind of thing?" His voice had a tinge of suspicion.

"We're on twenty-four hours in this department, sir. It's the only way to keep up."

"Oh." Suspicion remained in his voice.

"Besides," Kopriva said, "we catch a lot of people on the phone between five and ten PM. Everyone who works, basically. We generally try not to call after ten, though." He glanced at his watch. It was 10:08 PM. "Anyway, Mr. Belzer, you should have restored mail service immediately and receive all your misdirected mail within three days. If you have any problems, call the customer service department between eight and four and they'll help you."

"Okay. Thanks."

"Thank you, sir." Kopriva hung up. He looked at Katie.

"Stef," she said, "you are the king of bullshit."

"I had to think of something."

"No, it was beautiful. A work of art. Now what?"

Kopriva gave her the address. "We go get him."

"Meet you there."

The drive was a quick one. Kopriva felt good. Proper trickery was fun to use. He had acted in a couple of plays in high school and this was sort of the same thing, only here he had to ad-lib. The key was to keep it simple.

Belzer's Mom's house was smaller than Michelle's, but the yard was equally well-tended. Kopriva wondered if lawn care was a family fetish. He and Katie stole up to the house, and he peered in the window. A male sat in the easy chair watching TV. He couldn't tell if it was Belzer or not. He motioned for Katie to knock. As soon as she rapped on the door, the man stood and nonchalantly strolled to the door.

Kopriva smiled. It was him.

Kopriva stepped onto the porch and prepared to force the door back open if Belzer tried to close it once he saw who was on his doorstep. The door swung open and Belzer stared at them for a moment, obviously surprised. The faint odor of marijuana smoke wafted through the door.

"Martin? Can I come in and talk to you for a minute?" Kopriva played it low-key.

Belzer blinked at them, shocked. "Okay," he said and stepped aside to let them in.

As soon as they were in the door, Kopriva put him into a mild wrist-lock. Katie took the other arm. When he encountered no resistance, Kopriva made no attempt to use further force. He told Belzer he was under arrest.

"For what? I'm just watching TV."

"You have several warrants." Kopriva handcuffed him and began to search. Katie pulled a plastic bag from her pocket and held it for Belzer's possessions.

"What warrants? I thought I took care of those," Belzer said, not convincing anyone.

"Evidently not." Kopriva continued to search. He came across an orange-brown chunk wrapped in a baggy. "Uh-oh, Martin. What's this?"

"Crank," Belzer said dejectedly.

Kopriva hadn't expected an answer, but he didn't quibble. "Before I go any further, let me ask you something. Are there any needles on you? Because if I stick myself on a needle, I am going to be one ticked off hombre."

"They're in my sunglasses case. In my flannel pocket." Belzer stared straight ahead.

Kopriva pulled the case from Belzer's breast pocket. Inside, he saw two needles, a spoon, some cotton and some water in a small plastic bottle. "How long have you been shooting this stuff?"

"Too long, man."

Kopriva completed his search, then walked to the seat where Belzer had been sitting. An empty marijuana pipe lay on the small end table. Kopriva didn't see any marijuana nearby. He picked up the pipe, which was still warm. He put it to his nose and sniffed. The strong aroma of marijuana flooded his nostrils.

"Should I leave this for your Mom?" he asked
Belzer.

"No, man. It's mine. She doesn't need to know."

"I suppose not. Do you have keys for this place so
we can lock up?"

"They're in my jacket there by the door. Left
pocket."

Kopriva walked to the coat rack by the door and
picked up the heavy, black leather jacket.

"Left pocket," Belzer repeated. He watched
Kopriva intently.

Kopriva checked the left pocket and found a small
key ring.

"That's them," Belzer said quickly.

"You want this jacket?" Kopriva asked.

"No."

"No?"

Belzer shook his head. "No."

Kopriva began to search the jacket. Belzer sighed
and shifted his feet, nervously. Kopriva found
needles in the inside pocket and a small vial of
clear liquid.

"What's this?" he asked Belzer.

"Water."

"Water? Yeah, right. You're so nervous about me finding your needles and water."

"I'm not nervous about nothing, man. It's water."

"All right. Let's go. Do you want me to bring this jacket now?"

"What jacket? I never saw that jacket before in my life."

Kopriva shook his head with a rueful laugh. "Martin, you need to find another profession. You suck as a liar."

Belzer said nothing.

Kopriva locked the door as they left and walked Belzer to his car. Once he was secured in the back seat, Kopriva broke out his drug field test kits. Katie stood nearby, watching. A sliver from the methamphetamine chunk immediately flowed orange.

"Bingo," Kopriva muttered.

He tested a few drops of the "water" for methamphetamine with no reaction. "What do you think?" he asked Katie.

"It's not going to be heroin," she said with a shrug. "The only other drug I know that people shoot with needles is coke."

Kopriva retrieved a cocaine field test kit and dropped three drops into the vial. He broke the ampule inside. The vial flowed an instant, bright blue.

"Good call," he told Katie.

"Nice job. Especially on the bullshitting. You need any help with property or anything?"

Kopriva shook his head. "No. Thanks for coming along."

Katie nodded curtly, then turned and left. Kopriva watched her go. *Something was seriously wrong with her tonight.*

He started the car and headed for jail. Belzer leaned forward. "How'd you find me, anyway?"

"Martin, it's your mother's house. You think we wouldn't check there?"

Belzer didn't answer right away. After Kopriva pulled onto an arterial, Belzer asked, "Did you call me and pretend to be from the Post Office?"

"What?"

"Not five minutes before you came by, some guy from the Post Office called. Was that you?"

"No." Kopriva slowed for a red light. "What'd he want?"

"Just to get a forwarding address." Belzer watched him in the rear-view mirror. "I think it was you."

"Well, it wasn't."

"I think you're lying."

"Martin, using the Postal Service in any way to commit fraud against anyone is a federal offense. Great as your idea sounds, it would be illegal." He met Belzer's eyes in the mirror. "Why is it so hard for you to believe that we came to your Mom's house to see if you were there? Where would you check for someone with a warrant?"

"I suppose so. It just seems like one hell of a coincidence."

"Stranger things have happened."

"Yeah. But not to me."

The traffic light turned green. Kopriva nudged the accelerator, then shrugged at Belzer. "Life is full of surprises."

***

The Qwik-stop didn't get much business after 9:00 P.M. That suited Curly Pierson just fine. He could raid the magazine rack and read comics for free if there were no customers in the place. He especially liked the war comics. They reminded him of his eleven months in the Marine Corps. He often wished he hadn't had those problems that got him booted out, but he did okay now. Worked three days a week here and did some yard work for his mother. Played paint-ball on the weekends.

If the Corps had known how good he was at paint-ball, they would have begged him to stay, he thought without bitterness. He was the best on his team, even if he did play a little bit too emotionally intense. The doctor guy said he would probably be able to control it someday, especially if he kept up with the medication. He didn't like the pills, though. They made him tired.

Work bored him. Especially nights like this one. He'd read all the good comics, which of course were the DC ones, and the new ones wouldn't be in until the next day. He considered reading some of the Marvel comics if it got too slow, but what was the point of that? All those guys like Spiderman spent too much time worrying and wondering about stuff, even when they were fighting bad guys. Guys like Superman knew what was what. They were real heroes. Spiderman was a geek.

Curly stood behind the counter and fingered the .25 auto under the counter. It sat on the small shelf directly beneath the register. His boss had told him never to use it, but why did he keep it there, then? It wasn't like he didn't know how to handle a gun. He won two paintball matches just last weekend and both times he'd been the last man alive on his team.

He sighed and glanced at the comic book rack, then at the candy rack. He considered having a Snickers bar when a flash of movement near the door caught his eye.

Curly saw it for trouble before the guy even hit the door. He recognized the black hair down to the shoulders from the newspaper drawing and the scar seemed to leap right off the man's intense face. He reminded Curly, briefly, of his drill instructor at boot camp.

"The fucking money in a bag! Now!" The man even sounded like a drill sergeant. He leveled the small black revolver at Curly's face.

Scared, Curly slid the register drawer open. At the same moment, a thought occurred to him. A wonderful thought. A way to gain recognition. Maybe even get himself back into the Corps. To be a hero.

"Put the money in the fucking bag, you little geek!" The man screamed, out of control. Curly figured that as a good thing. Those that didn't keep their heads always lost at paint-ball.

Curly put all the bills into a paper bag and slid the register closed. Using the bag to cover his movement, he reached under the register and grasped the .25 auto.

"Free—" he started to say, bringing the gun up. He felt a sharp pain in his cheek and heard a muffled roar. Everything slowed down. He tried to squeeze the trigger but couldn't. He saw a flash of light and felt a pin-prick in his abdomen. The floor rushed up and caught him, leaving him sprawled on his back. He watched the man jump over the counter and take the bag from his hand.

He blinked.

The man was gone.

He blinked again, staring at the alarm button. He willed it to depress itself. The button sat motionless, a stoic accusation.

You blew it, it said. *You blew it in the Corps and you are no hero, Curly.*

He tried to blink again, but found he could not open his eyes after he had closed them.

Thursday, August 22nd
Graveyard Shift

A gang meant family, plain and simple. It provided
what kids either didn't have in their own families
or just didn't want from them. Until people
realized that, they would never understand the
power of the gangs. It was about being a part of
something. Being *accepted*.

Gerald Anthony Trellis did everything he could to
be black. He talked like the gangsters, dressed like
them, walked like them. He listened to rap. Most of
all, he cursed his white skin, an accident of birth.
He knew what some of the racist white boys in
River City called him—*wigger*. White nigger.
They meant it as an insult, but he accepted the
word with a measure of pride, even though it was
the only thing that kept him from being fully
accepted.

In a way, he should be thankful that he was from
River City. Demographics forced the Compton
Crips to allow whites into their gang activity. And
Trellis, who called himself T-Dog, was the number
one recruit of Morris the Cat.

Morris lay on T-Dog's couch with earphones on,
listening to one of T-Dog's many rap CD's. T-Dog
gave Morris pretty much anything he wanted. He
had the juice here in the RC, and held T-Dog's
ticket to full acceptance. Plus, The Cat liked him.
Only last week he had mentioned sponsoring him
down to Compton to get beat in.

Man, to get beat in by a Compton Crip set! T-Dog

felt a rush of pride. His whole life, everyone told him what a loser he was. His father, when he showed up, just beat on him. His mother had all these stupid rules she expected him to follow. School wasn't for him, either. Why should he sit politely in class and listen to some adult when he made more money working with Morris than they did? How many 17-year-olds could afford a brand new car?

The Crips gave him power and he liked it. Morris would make sure he got beat in, giving him even more power.

The thing was, though, Morris had been pretty distracted and pissed off lately. He hadn't mentioned the beat-in for over a week. He spent all his time bitching about everything, especially that white cop who busted him. T-Dog had never seen Morris so enraged. After he picked him up at jail that night, Morris screamed for almost an hour. Most of what he said hadn't made much sense. Something about what the other guys in the car were going to say about the way that cop treated him.

T-Dog knew he wasn't as smart as Morris. The guy was in charge not only because of his juice but also because of his brains. But T-Dog started to formulate a small plan, one that would satisfy Morris' rage and give them both some juice. Maybe even enough to get him beat in.

After all, where could he get the ultimate juice?

***

Eyes droopy and his breathing shallow, James

Mace sat in the small chair in the corner of the apartment bedroom. On the floor beside him he'd discarded the small needle that had delivered all three of them to this land of floating stillness. A bent and burnt spoon lay on the nightstand next to a wet, deflated cotton ball.

Mace blinked slowly, forcing his eyes to open again. He knew his face was expressionless, but he imagined himself with a broad, satisfied smile.

Things were getting worse. He couldn't even enjoy his fix any more. It was like taking aspirin now, taking away his itches, aches and nausea. His skin and clothing were disgustingly dirty, but he didn't care. It kept the drug inside longer and besides, cleanliness was overrated.

He looked at the bed. Leslie and Andrea, both nude, lay motionless, their limbs wrapped around each other. He wished that he had more than a passing drive for sex. He hadn't slept with either of them for weeks. He didn't care that they were occasionally doing each other in his absence. Both of them were worthless, anyway. On the last two hits, he had to call another whore, Carla, to drive. Crack-head Carla. She worked cheap and quickly realized that driving a car was more profitable and less dangerous than hooking.

He'd banged Carla twice last week, more to subjugate her than for any real need for sex. A woman was more easily controlled once you'd screwed her. Made 'em loyal. At least Carla had shown a little more enthusiasm than Leslie or Andrea had in a long while.

Being the man was hard, Mace groused from the

depths of his floating world. He had to be responsible for everything. Even in the midst of what should have been his euphoria, he was thinking of his next fix and how he would relax during that one.

His thoughts drifted to the last robbery. God*damn* that had been sweet. That goofy little clerk tried to pull a gun on him, and he fucking wasted the little geek. Blew a hole right in his cheek and pumped another one into his gut. That had been the greatest thrill Mace had experienced since Panama. The power rush was incredible. It made him feel alive. Hell, he needed the heroin just to come down from that high.

His eyes drooped closed and he took a deep breath. When he opened them, he saw the women were awake. Leslie gently stroked Andrea along the curve of her hip. Mace felt no stirring in his loins at the sight. He thought instead of his next fix. More than that, he thought about how he would get the money.

And how good it was going to feel to take out the enemy.

***

Stefan Kopriva awoke feeling he had forgotten something. Everything seemed normal, but he knew there was something out of sync.

Then he saw Katie McLeod lying next to him, felt her soft breath on his shoulder.

Kopriva almost jumped in surprise as the events of the previous night came rushing back to him. He willed himself to lie still while he recalled everything that had happened. It reminded him of being drunk and forgetting everything in the morning. Only he had not been drinking.

After he had finished booking Belzer and putting the drugs on property, a homicide had been called in. Both of them guarded the crime scene all night at the Qwik-stop where a twenty-some-year-old clerk had been shot, probably by Scarface. Katie's demeanor hadn't changed from earlier in the night. After the scene was secured, they'd gone to breakfast for their seven and she finally told him. Her fiancée had broken up with her after fourteen months of engagement and three and a half years together. With no explanation.

Stef, you are a jerk, he told himself.

He and McLeod went through the Academy together and, for whatever reason, that gave them a bond that made talking easier. After the shift secured, they went out for coffee and talked some more. Katie seemed to relax a little more once they were out of uniform. When she became upset, Kopriva offered to take her home. She'd wanted to talk some more. Kopriva lived not too far from the coffee shop, so they'd gone there for tea and to continue talking.

Katie broke down and cried before Kopriva had even gotten the hot water for tea on the stove. Through her tears, he gathered that she thought she'd loved her fiancée, but now wasn't so sure. It hurt to be dumped but there might there also be a sense of relief.

Kopriva understood some of what she felt. His

luck with women bordered on abysmal. He hated one-night stands, but had been involved in little else for the past year. He knew what hurt felt like.

Around 9:00 A.M., tired, cried out and grateful, Katie had leaned into him for a comforting hug, which he happily gave.

Carefully, Stef. Her breath plumed lightly against his shoulder. He shifted his position and tried to get comfortable. It didn't work.

How did it really happen?

He hadn't intended for anything to happen. Had he? He remembered that he kissed the top of her head and told her everything would be all right. He remembered how warm she felt against him and how good her hair smelled. Katie looked up and smiled a tired, friendly smile.

Thanks, Stef. That's what she had said. And she kissed him softly on the cheek. She started to withdraw her face, then paused. Kopriva remembered that the silence then had been a loud one. Then she kissed his cheek again, softer and closer to his lips.

He kissed her on the mouth and they melted into each other.

Now it was almost 6 P.M., and she was lying next to him. The smell of sex hung over the bed like an accusation. He'd taken advantage of her, hadn't he?

Kopriva shut the alarm off so that it wouldn't wake her. He slipped out of bed and walked down the hall to the bathroom. As he stepped into the shower, his mind whirred with a confused jumble of images. He could see her crying at the coffee shop. Then he saw her athletic body beneath him, her back arching as they made love.

Kopriva forced the image from his mind.

This was a mistake. He'd taken advantage of a woman while she was hurt and rejected.

But there'd always been something between them. Maybe this just provided the opportunity for it to come out.

He and Katie always had chemistry, even back at the Academy. Since then, they'd been assigned to separate sectors on patrol. Both worked the north side all year and units were often called on to cross Division. Kopriva enjoyed her friendship but had never considered anything beyond that. She was always dating someone, then got engaged. Honor might have been an out-dated concept for some, but Kopriva adhered to it. It was his lifeboat in a sea of madness sometimes.

Had he just violated it?

Fifteen minutes later, Kopriva shut off the shower. No, he realized, he had not violated honor. What had happened wasn't a mistake. Only the timing had been and that was over now. He saw this as a good thing, but one they should probably keep from their co-workers.

Kopriva toweled off and slipped on a pair of boxer shorts. He decided that he would make her breakfast. During breakfast he would let her know that he hoped this was the beginning of something nice.

He walked into the kitchen and removed a frying pan from the cupboard. He began warming it on the stove. In the fridge, he had enough eggs for an omelet. He removed the eggs along with a little cheese and some green onions. As the pan heated up, he walked to the bedroom to wake her in case she wanted to shower before she ate.

But the bed lay empty with rumpled covers. Her clothes were gone.

***

Lieutenant Robert Saylor didn't have to order the graveyard patrol shift to pay attention. As soon as he stepped behind the lectern of the roll-call room, conversation quickly tapered off.

He put aside a couple of stolen vehicle reports for later, then reviewed the homicide at the Qwik-stop from the night before.

"That's the big news, folks," Saylor said. "The guy day shift nabbed was a copy-cat."

"No kidding," James Kahn muttered.

"Yeah," Saylor said. "No kidding. Well, that also comes from the detectives at Major Crimes, who interviewed day shift's guy. He is *not* Scarface. The M.O. he used was similar but not exact. The funny thing is, it was exactly the M.O. the paper published."

That brought a few chuckles from the assembled troops.

"Imagine that," Chisolm said to no one in particular.

"Yeah," said Saylor. "So if Scarface killed the clerk from last night, then he is obviously getting more dangerous. Be careful. Think about how you want to pursue him, whether on foot or in a vehicle. First officer on scene is in charge, I don't care if it is the newest recruit we got. Until a sergeant or myself can get on scene and be briefed, the first one on scene is site commander."

Saylor glanced down at his notes. "The clerk evidently pulled a gun, so maybe Scarface won't kill unless provoked. But who knows, so be careful."

Saylor moved briskly through the stolen reports and several other less important items then turned things over to the sergeants for their platoon meetings. He took a seat at the Adam Sector table.

Sgt. Shen repeated Saylor's warning. "I would rather this guy get away than one of you get killed," he said. "Do what you have to do, but be careful."

The Adam Sector troops nodded in response.

Shen pointed to his right. "For everyone who doesn't know him, this is Officer Jack Willow, who just graduated from the Academy. He went to the Seattle Academy on the west side of the state and not ours, so be patient with him." Shen grinned as the group chuckled. "Welcome aboard, Officer Willow."

Jack Willow cleared his throat. "Uh, thanks, Sergeant."

Willow's FTO, Officer Aaron Norris, sat to the recruit's left. "Don't get too used to his face." He offered a sly smile. "They sent him to the axe-man first, so I could save the department some money in the long run."

"Hey, what's your shirt size, kid?" James Kahn asked. "I'll buy it off you cheap when they send you packing."

Everyone chuckled, except for Willow, who gave one nervous burst of laughter and then looked around the table.

"All right, enough," Shen said with a grin. "You'll give the boy a complex." He dismissed the platoon.

Saylor told Shen that he'd be at a meeting for the early part of the shift. "Hart is forming some sort of task force, and I'm supposed to give my input."

Shen remained politically silent.

"I'd say I wouldn't be long," Saylor added, "but the Captain will be there and you know how he likes the sound of his own voice."

Shen struggled not to smile. "Call me for coffee when you're clear?"

"You got it."

***

Katie MacLeod drove slowly along the residential street, glancing around, her eyes never still. Everything she saw registered in her mind, but being pre-occupied, it had little impact on her. She felt out of sorts. Embarrassed, actually. It hadn't really been fair of her to slip out of Kopriva's bed like that and slink home without a word. It made her feel like a slut.

But what was she supposed to do? She'd been upset and he had comforted her. It's not like he took advantage, but things might not have happened if she hadn't been so upset about breaking up with Kevin.

"Oh, who are you kidding?" she said aloud. She and Kopriva had always had some sexual tension. She'd just never acted on it.

So what to do now? Katie sighed. She liked him. She would like to see him, but things had moved so fast. Then she ran out on him. Who knows what he thought about her now?

Besides, cop-on-cop relationships were difficult at best. Maybe she should buy him a cup of coffee and explain that they should just stay friends. After all, they had a good friendship and romance always messed that up.

But she couldn't do that, could she? Not with the feeling in her stomach right now. All that pent up emotion ever since the Academy had burst free, and she couldn't just put the genie back in the bottle.

Pent up emotion? Or rebound? Some of her affection for Kopriva was real, she knew that, but maybe the intensity came from being dumped. Possibly. Probably. Hell, she knew it did.

Katie sighed and tapped the steering wheel. She

was on the rebound and acted like a slut with a decent looking guy who happened to be nice. The guy had a chance to get laid and took it.

No harm done, but no great love affair, either, she realized.

Cut it off, Katie. Just cut it off before it ruins—

"*Adam-116, Adam-112,*" the dispatcher's voice broke into her thoughts.

"Adam-116, go ahead."

"*Adam-112, go,*" came Chisolm's calm voice.

"*Adam-116, Adam-112, a domestic at 2114 W. Swanson. Complainant is a neighbor who wishes to remain anonymous. Complainant states that the man and woman who live at the address have been yelling loudly for the last fifteen minutes. We have no listing for the occupants of that address. 2114 W. Swanson, a domestic.*"

"Copy."

"*Copy.*"

Katie drove quickly but carefully to the call, using Belt Street, a residential arterial. Every time she went to a domestic, she felt a brief pang in her stomach, even after three years of police work. She remembered her mother and father and how the police never came no matter how loud the screaming became. Or how much hitting occurred. Things were different in today's world, thank God.

She arrived at the house before Chisolm, parked a

ways off and approached. The house, a small blue cracker-box, sat on a tiny lot. The scraggly upkeep of the lawn and the 1976 Monza parked out front screamed rental to her. She slipped through the fence gate, hoping there were no dogs or dog piles in the small yard. Once on the porch, she moved quietly to the side of the front door and stood next to it, listening. She couldn't hear yelling inside, though there seemed to be some movement. She waited for Chisolm to arrive.

Katie stared at the crack in the porch, following it as it spider-webbed across the entire porch. This house had seen some hard years. She wondered what the people inside would look like.

She heard a creak of leather and looked up to see Chisolm standing behind her at the foot of the steps. She forced herself not to jump in surprise. Chisolm grinned, his portable radio in his hand. "Adam-112, on scene," he said in a muted tone, then slid the radio back into its holder on his belt.

"Pretty sneaky," Katie whispered.

"Silent and Invisible Deployment," Chisolm quoted from the Patrol Procedures Manual, still grinning.

Katie smiled back. "No talking inside. Just a little movement."

Chisolm nodded. "A house this size, rolling over in bed would shake the whole thing."

He stepped onto the porch and knocked on the door. There was a long pause, then a male voice asked, "Who is it?"

"Police," Chisolm said in an authoritative voice. He gave Katie a wink. "Open the door, sir."

Another pause and a muffled, "shit." Then the door opened and a white male stood inside the entryway. The first thing Katie noticed was his size. The man was huge and obviously a body-builder. A white T-shirt hugged his muscular chest. Cut off sleeves revealed bulging biceps and massive forearms, which bore the faded blue color of jailhouse tattoos. The man towered over Katie by almost a foot and had several inches on Chisolm. She guessed him to be six-foot-three, at least.

"Come on in," he said, his voice neutral.

Katie and Chisolm entered the small house. "Who else is here, sir?" Katie asked.

"Just my girlfriend."

"She lives here with you?"

"Yeah." The man's voice remained neutral.

"What exactly is going on tonight, sir?" Katie asked him.

A shrill female voice broke into the room. "I'll tell you what's going on here. He beat the shit out of me, that's what!"

Katie turned to see a blonde-haired woman about five feet tall standing in the doorway to the bedroom. She couldn't have weighed more than a hundred pounds.

"I'll talk with her," Katie told Chisolm, and moved toward the woman. As she drew closer, she immediately noticed a red handprint on her right cheek. "Let's talk in here, ma'am," Katie said, motioning to the bedroom.

The woman stomped into the small room. Katie followed.

"What's your name, ma'am?"

"Julie. Julie Krivner."

Katie jotted the name into her pocket notebook.

"Date of birth?"

"What does that matter? I'm the victim here. Are you going to arrest that animal out there?" Julie's voice rose shrilly.

Katie maintained an even voice. "Ma'am, we'll do a complete investigation and if an arrest is in order, we will make it."

"That sounds like cop bullshit to me. I want him in jail and *I want him in jail now!*" she shrieked.

"Relax, ma'am."

"Relax?!" Julie's voice exploded into a screech. "Don't you tell me to relax. I was just beaten by that asshole in there. Now do your fucking job and arrest him!"

Katie struggled to keep her voice calm and held an open palm in front of the woman's face. "Ma'am, that's not how it works. We have to interview—"

"Oh, I see. You come in here and see his big arms and your little heart goes all mushy." Julie put her hands on her hips. "You're pathetic."

Katie's jaw clenched. "Listen to me! I don't want your boyfriend. I am only here to investigate—"

"Oh, you don't want him? So you're a lez-bo, is that it? You probably want me, then."

"No." Katie said in a clipped tone. "I don't. Now what happened here tonight?"

"I don't want to talk to any lez-bos."

"Fine."

Katie stepped out of the room. Chisolm and the body-builder both stared at her.

"Tom? You want to—"

"Sure."

Jesus, everyone is interrupting me tonight. Katie strode toward the man as Chisolm brushed past her. She asked his name.

"It's Steve."

"Last name?"

"Marino. Like the quarterback."

"You're birth date?"

"November 22, 1967."

"Do you work, sir?"

Steve nodded. "Yes, ma'am. I work construction as a laborer for Greenwood Builders."

"Okay, Steve. What happened here tonight?"

"Officer, I'm sorry for the way she's acting. She just—"

Katie interrupted, taking a brief pleasure in finally being the one to cut in. "It's all right, Steve. Just tell me what happened."

Steve took a deep breath and let out a huge sigh. "I can't go to jail, officer."

"No one said you were going to jail. We just have to find out what happened."

"No, you don't understand. I'm on parole. If I go to jail for any reason, my parole will be revoked and I'll go back to Walla Walla for three years." He took another huge breath and let it out. Every muscle in his upper body tensed and released as he stared at the wall.

Katie felt a stab of fear. If he decided to fight—

Just work the call, Katie. "Steve, let's worry about one thing at a time, okay?" She used her professional, but soothing tone.

"I can't go back to the Walls, man," Steve said. He trembled slightly and Katie watched his eyes tear up. "I'll die before I'll go back."

"Steve? Take it easy, okay? It'll be all right."

Steve didn't respond.

"Steve? One thing at a time, okay? We'll work it out, you and me."

Steve gave a nod.

"Good. Now tell me what happened."

Steve let out another huge breath. "We've been together about eleven years. About nine years ago, I got in a bar-fight and killed a guy. They sent me up for first-degree manslaughter. I got nine years for that. Can you believe that? Nine years for defending myself in a bar-fight?"

"Sounds unfair," Katie said calmly.

Steve looked at her, as if gauging her sincerity. Then he nodded. "Yeah. It was. I did six years as a model prisoner and made parole. Jules stuck by me the whole time. Or so I thought."

"What's that mean?"

Steve shrugged. "Lately, she's been hounding me about everything. I don't make enough money. She might have to go to work, says she's tired of working after six years. She complains about the time I spend at the gym, too."

"You spend a lot of time there?"

"Yeah," Steve admitted. "Three hours a day, after work. But that is all I do. I work and I go work out at the gym, then I come home. I don't go out drinking, nothing."

"So why is she upset?"

"She's not. I am."

"Why?"

Steve let out another huge sigh. "I found out tonight she's been sleeping with my best friend since I went away to prison. I pretty much caught them today."

"You caught them in the act?"

"Not exactly. I wasn't feeling too good today, so I skipped my workout. When I pulled up, my buddy was driving away from the house. When I came inside, she was still in the bed. Plus, I could…it was in the air." He looked down at his feet.

Katie didn't know what to say. She waited for him to continue.

After a moment, he said, "We avoided each other for about an hour, but eventually we started arguing. She blamed it on me. I told her she was a whore." He looked up at Katie. "I didn't mean it. Or maybe I did. I don't know. She flew off the handle and started kicking me and hitting me. Then she called me a faggot. She said I probably liked it in the pen because I could have all the guys I wanted. Stuff like that."

"She hit you?"

Steve nodded.

"Did she leave any marks?"

Steve gave her a look. "She's five-foot, ninety-five pounds. What do you think?"

"I have to ask."

"No. No marks."

"All right. Then what happened?"

"I got mad. I have a bad temper. It takes me a while to get mad, but then I just explode. When she started saying that stuff about being a faggot, I just lost control, you know? I mean, I fought guys off for six years. I never got broke." He pointed to one of the tattoos on his forearm. "See that? BSC. Brotherhood of the Southern Cross. I had to hook up with the asshole Aryan bikers to stay alive in there. You think it's easy being around those racist bastards?"

Katie shook her head. "I doubt it."

"It ain't easy at all," he told her, "but it kept me from having to deal with a lot worse shit. I never punked out to anyone, not in six years. Then she goes and calls me a faggot."

"I can understand that making you mad. Did you hit her then?"

Steve nodded. "Yeah, I did. I slapped her."

"Once?"

"Yes. Just once. I even used my left hand."

"Did anything else physical happen?"

"No. She ran into the bedroom, and I sat down in the chair. Then you guys showed up." Steve's shoulders slumped and he looked at the floor.

174

"Katie?" Chisolm was at her elbow.

There was nowhere else to move so they could confer privately, so they had to speak in codes.

"What do you have, Tom?"

Chisolm glanced at Steve, who was still staring at his shoes. He then tapped his cheek and motioned to Julie. "One-Edward," he said quietly, using the radio clearance code for an arrest and booking. He nodded toward Steve.

Katie nodded. "Same here."

Steve looked up at them. His calm demeanor was slipping. "Look, man. I know the law. You're going to arrest me. But I told you, if I go to jail, my parole is revoked. I am not going back to the Walls. No way."

"Steve," Katie soothed, "maybe your parole officer will give you a break."

"That prick? Not a chance."

Katie noted the intensity of Steve's words. She considered requesting further backup, but didn't want to tip him over. She sensed Chisolm's presence behind her.

"You belong in prison!" Julie piped up. "Faggot woman-beater."

"Be quiet!" Katie told her.

"Don't tell me what to do in my own house, you dyke!" Julie shot back.

Katie turned away from her. "Steve, listen. I know you're not a criminal. Don't be one now."

"I'm not. I'm not a criminal," Steve said, his voice tight. He stood up straight, his arms rigid.

Oh, Jesus, Katie thought. *He's getting ready to fight.*

"I know you're not," she kept trying. "You were only defending yourself six years ago. Tonight you just lost your temper for a minute."

"I can't go back," Steve said, not listening to her. He swayed slightly with adrenaline. Katie could sense Chisolm moving forward slowly. She wondered briefly if they would have to kill him.

"Steve, listen to me. You can't win—"

"You can never win!" Julie yelled. "You're a goddamn loser, and you belong in prison, faggot!"

Katie shifted her legs as casually as she could, assuming a defensive stance and hoping it wasn't obvious. She didn't take her eyes off of Steve. His jaw clenched and his eyes darted from Julie to Chisolm to Katie and back to Julie again. His hands balled into fists.

"You." Chisolm's deep voice was deadly as he spoke to Julie. "Be quiet."

Katie blinked, surprised when Julie obeyed. She didn't have time to marvel at that, though. "Steve," she said, trying to keep her voice even, "you can't win here if you fight. We have a dozen cops on the way. We have mace, nightsticks and guns. One

176

way or another, you will be arrested. Then your parole officer will get a report that you resisted arrest, maybe even assaulted an officer, and he will definitely revoke you."

Katie swallowed. If he planned to fight, she only had a few seconds left to talk him out of it. Chisolm stood beside her, silent. She pushed ahead, keeping her voice reasonable and soothing.

"If you go willingly, Steve, I can write in my report that you were not only honest, but entirely cooperative. When your P.O. reads that and you explain the rest of the circumstances, he might not revoke you."

"He will. He hates me."

"He might not."

"He will." Steve's voice sounded dead now. "I'm not going back."

"Steve, I will even call him and explain things on your behalf. That might sway him, right?"

Steve studied her, his eyes softening slightly.

Katie continued. "Look at the situation. You're working hard, you work out, you don't drink, right? She is the one who is treating you like hell. She cheated on you. Anyone would get mad. It's understandable. It wasn't right to hit her. You know that and so do I, but it isn't something that you should go back to prison for. If you fight us, though, that is definitely where you will go. If you cooperate here, I can put all that in my report. I can call your P.O. We can work things out."

She watched him carefully.

"It's your only chance, Steve."

Steve stared at her intently throughout her entire speech. A long, tense moment of silence followed.

It didn't work. He's going to fight and someone is going to die.

When he spoke, he spoke carefully, the edge out of his voice. "You'd really call him and explain?"

Katie let out an inward sigh. "Yes. Absolutely."

Steve sighed, then nodded slowly. "Okay. What do you want me to do?"

Katie directed him to turn around and quickly handcuffed him. It required two pairs of handcuffs linked together because of his size and broad back. The small, silver cuffs looked frail on his large wrists. Katie imagined that he could snap them if he wished.

"Steve, you made the right decision," she told him.

"I hope so."

"Is that how it works?" Julie chirped at Katie. "You are all willing to go to bat for a woman-beater?"

"Did you ever hit her before tonight, Steve?" Katie asked him quietly.

"No. Never."

Katie turned to Julie. "He said you hit him tonight, too, Julie."

"I did not. He's a lying ex-con."

"Has he ever hit you before, Julie?"

"Yes. All the time. I am a battered woman."

"What you are is a cheater who got caught," Katie told her stiffly.

"We're not married!"

Katie stared at her, disbelieving.

Steve spoke up, his voice neutral again. "Officer, can we go? I'd like to leave and never come back here again."

"Sure." Katie led him toward the door.

"YOU FAGGOT!" Julie screamed.

Steve stopped, turned his head slightly and said in the same even voice, "My mother was right about you, Julie. You're just a little bitch."

Julie gave a shocked sound.

"I agree," Katie said, and led Steve out the door.

"I heard that, you dyke! I am going to file a complaint! What's your badge number?" She tried to follow them, but Chisolm stopped her.

"Ma'am," he said in the same flat voice he had used before. "You might want to shut that sewer of yours, or I will take his word for it and arrest you for assault. Then you can make that complaint from jail. You understand me?"

Katie grinned at Julie's silence.

"Good," Chisolm said. "Now go back inside and close your door."

Katie heard a moment of silence, the scuffle of feet, then a loud slam.

"I'm glad someone can shut her up," Steve muttered.

Katie struggled not to laugh. Not only was the situation perversely funny to her, but the relief of stress from a few moments ago made her giddy. She barely managed to hold her laughter inside.

She reached her patrol car, searched Steve and put him in the back seat. When she closed the door, Chisolm appeared beside her again.

"Jesus, Tom, will you stop sneaking up on me?" she joked.

Chisolm grinned for a moment, then turned serious. "Well done," he said with a nod. "Very well done." Then he turned and walked toward his car.

"Thanks," Katie said. She watched him go and felt a flush of pride. Chisolm was one of the most respected street officers on the department, if not *the* most. He didn't throw compliments around lightly.

Katie slid into the driver's seat of her patrol car. She felt good.

"Officer?"

Katie glanced at Steve in the rear-view mirror. "Yes?"

"Thanks."

Katie nodded. "Okay, Steve. We'll work it out."

Steve nodded, then stared out the window.

Katie started the car and headed toward the jail. Despite her elation at the success of the call and Chisolm's compliment, it ranked as quite possibly the longest trip to jail she'd ever made.

***

Kopriva waited restlessly for the data channel to return his driver's check. The car in front of him wasn't a maggot car, but the woman blew through the light at Division and Indiana right in front of him, so he stopped her. Usually, he would have let her go with a warning.

Usually.

But tonight he was grumpy.

Katie had not even looked his way all through roll call. He watched for her down in the sally-port as he waited for a car, hoping to make a plan to get coffee at two or three in the morning, once things slowed down, but she didn't show up before he had to leave.

"Baker-123."

Kopriva clicked the mike, an informal response that most dispatchers frowned upon. Janice manned the data channel, and she didn't mind.

"Wilson is not in locally. DOL is clear through 1998 with lenses."

Kopriva clicked the mike again. He'd already written the ticket for failing to stop for a steady red light. He exited his vehicle and approached Wilson. The date on her driver's license put her at forty-three, but she looked ten years younger, dressed in slacks and a business-like blouse. He hadn't smelled any alcohol on her breath and figured she just worked late.

Or maybe she was fooling around with some guy. Who knows?

"Mrs. Wilson," he recited, "this is a notice of infraction for failing to stop at a steady red light at Division and Indiana. Please sign here. It is not an admission of guilt, only a promise to respond within fifteen days." He held out the ticket book and a pen.

"But that light was yellow," she protested, not reaching for the proffered ticket book.

"It was red, ma'am."

"Well, I would like to tell you my side of the story."

"Ma'am, I don't care about your side of the story. You failed to stop for the light. I am citing you.

Please sign." Kopriva did not raise his voice.

"That isn't fair," she told him. Her eyes narrowed and her face tightened.

"Ma'am, one of your options is to go to court and tell the judge your side of the story."

"No. I won't sign it."

Kopriva paused, staring at her.

"I won't sign it," she repeated.

Kopriva suppressed a sigh. "Ma'am, if you do not sign this, I will write you a criminal citation for failing to sign a notice of infraction. If you refuse to sign that, you will be booked into jail."

She looked at him, obviously shocked at the word 'jail.' "Oh, that is just ridiculous."

"It's the law."

She considered, and then reached for the ticket book. She angrily scrawled her name on the ticket. "I want your name and badge number," she insisted.

"It's on the ticket," Kopriva told her, handing her the driver's copy. He walked briskly back to his car.

Sitting behind the wheel, he shut off the spotlight with his left hand and punched the button for the bright take-down lights on top of the car, killing them as well. The woman signaled, paused and pulled out into traffic. Kopriva slid the ticket in the visor above him.

He didn't feel any better.

He reached for his mike to clear the stop when a shrill tone broke over his radio.

***

Patrol Captain Michael Reott sat at the head of the table. He'd just finished a short introduction outlining what he hoped to see any task force accomplish. He also covered some of the pitfalls he hoped such an endeavor would avoid. Lt. Hart, Lt. Saylor and Sgt. Michaels occupied seats at the table with him. Michaels sat in for the vacationing Lt. PowellPowell.

"So what options do we have?" Reott said, signaling that he'd finished talking for awhile.

Hart pounced on the opportunity. "Sir, the media is skewering us over this. We need to be high profile on this task force. Back them off a little bit."

Reott paused, considering the logic.

Saylor disagreed. "Cap, the newspaper is going to bash on us no matter what. That's a given, but the television media has been pretty fair. I mean, the guy has gotten away with how many armed robberies? Fourteen, fifteen?"

"Fifteen," Hart supplied.

"Fifteen, then. Plus, he's shot at cops and now he's killed a guy."

"What's your point, Rob?" Reott asked.

"The point is we have to get this sonofabitch before he kills someone else. Telling everyone that we are forming a task force takes away the element of surprise. If he watches TV and sees a news report, he'll be more cautious. We need to capitalize on his carelessness."

Reott considered, but did not commit. "What about the copy-cats?"

Hart jumped in. "A highly publicized effort on our part will deter further copy-cats. They will be too afraid of getting caught."

"What's to fear?" Saylor asked. "This guy is fifteen-for-fifteen."

"And the only copy-cat is oh-for-one," Hart shot back.

Saylor shrugged. "Even so, you can expect more copy-cats the longer this goes. Which is why we have to shut this guy down."

Reott looked at Michaels, who gave a shrug. "We need to catch him, that's all I know."

Hart spoke up again. "My plan is to ask for volunteers during the hours Scarface has hit the most, eighteen hundred to zero two hundred hours. Seven total cars. Five cars will sit off on particular stores. We'll rotate which ones throughout the shift. At the same time, two cars will cruise between the five selected stores as a mobile response to augment patrol. Radio silence is to be observed. All units will use their regular call signs if they have to break radio silence. A code-word will be used, which will be given out at roll-call. If a surveilling unit sees a robbery shaping up, they get on the air, call the code-word and location. Instead of a time-delay, we get started before the robbery is even completed."

He leaned back, pleased with his plan.

Saylor nodded his approval. "It's a good plan. The unit on surveillance has to be extra careful, though, as far as engaging the suspect. Keeping a visual on him would be best, even if he gets out of the store before patrol arrives. At least this way, we might get a good perimeter set up and force him to go to ground. Then we could bring in the K-9 for a track."

Reott pursed his lips. "Okay, but do you foresee any liability issues with that unit basically watching a robbery take place?"

"No," both lieutenants responded simultaneously. Saylor motioned for Hart to continue.

"It's a matter of officer safety, sir," Hart told him. "We can't expect a plain-clothes officer to engage an armed robber with no back-up. We might take some heat, but we'd come out all right."

Reott mulled over Hart's explanation for a few moments, then looked at all three and continued. "I think we'll go with Alan's plan. It's a good one. Choose your people and brief them carefully. I'll okay the overtime with the Chief."

"And the media?" Hart asked.

"Let's keep this quiet unless it gets found out. Then we'll invite them in and give them the inside scoop if they keep it quiet until we catch the guy. Make 'em an ally for once."

Saylor and Hart both nodded. Reott congratulated himself on his diplomatic abilities.

The phone rang. Michaels, being the junior man, automatically answered it. He listened for a few seconds, then replaced the receiver.

"He just hit again. Number sixteen. Time delay is only two minutes."

Damn, Reott thought, then, "Okay, Gentleman. That's the plan. Do whatever it takes to catch this guy. You have my full support."

Interlude
Fall 1994

"I don't really believe in counseling, doc. That's all."

"Why is that?" The doctor kept any hint of disapproval out of his voice.

"I think that it is the refuge of the weak. A man should be able to deal with his own demons."

"And a woman?"

"Same thing."

The doctor paused, considering. Thirty minutes had passed in the session and although the officer had begun to open up, little had been accomplished. He always had the option of requiring further sessions, but he knew full well how the administrators at the Police Department would interpret that. Still, the officer's mental health rated as his primary concern, not his law enforcement career.

"Every man is an island, then?" he asked the officer.

The officer nodded. "Who can you truly count on? I've been hung out to dry before."

"Beginning when?" Perhaps a look at the officer's childhood would reveal something noteworthy.

The officer didn't bite. "Let's just say I learned to fend for myself a long time ago and leave it at that, all right?"

The doctor didn't push the matter, though clearly something existed there. He returned to the previous point.

"In your profession, you are required to help a variety of different people, correct? Many of whom are undeserving or whose irresponsibility has caused the situation which you now must deal with. Am I right?"

The officer nodded. "Very accurate."

"Say there is a woman. She is very young, gets married. Her husband is abusive, but she won't or can't leave him. Maybe she has caused the situation or maybe she hasn't, but now she is stuck. He hits her. You come to the scene and arrest the husband for assault. She is now free to take action. She is no longer a prisoner of her own fear. There is a window of opportunity for her, and it is your action that empowered her. Is this accurate as well, officer?"

"Yes. Sometimes."

"Was it wrong of you to help her?"

"No."

"Wrong of her to accept your assistance?"

"Absolutely not."

"So now she can face her own demons." The doctor leaned back and watched the officer's face.

The officer remained impassive. Finally, he sighed. "I see your point."

"Good."

"So you want to hear something?"

"Of course."

"I'm a little angry at the administration. They haven't stood by me very well. And I did nothing wrong."

The doctor detected bitterness in the officer's voice. He could also sense a great deal more under the surface, but he expected that and didn't see a problem with it.

"Go on."

"Nothing more to say on that, doc. They should have been calling a press conference and damning the newspaper for the accusations it made. Instead, they open an IA investigation? And do you know the questions they asked me in IA? They all but called me a racist and a dirty cop. It's one thing coming from the jackals at the newspaper. It's something else entirely when it comes from your own agency." The officer shook his head. "I did my job and this is my thanks."

"But you are here."

"So?"

"So you do not intend to resign over it."

The officer paused. "Probably not. Maybe." He

sighed heavily. "I don't know."

The doctor watched him for several long moments as the officer stared at his own shoes. He cast a surreptitious glance at his watch and decided to get to the heart of the matter.

"Tell me about the man you killed, officer."

The officer looked up then, steel and fury in his eyes. "He tried to kill me. He's dead. What else do you want to know?"

Friday, August 23rd
Graveyard Shift

Katie MacLeod walked along the row of cars
parked in the basement and tossed her black
equipment bag onto the front seat of the police
patrol car assigned to her. She withdrew her
flashlight and placed it in the charger/holder right
below the radio. Her side-handle baton went into
the small holder in the driver's door, where she had
to wedge it in to keep it from falling out while
driving. She then seat-belted the equipment bag
into the passenger's seat, leaving the pockets with
her logbook, ticket books and report notebook
accessible without unbelting the bag.

She took a quick walk around the exterior to check
for any damage, finding nothing but dirt. Using the
button located in the driver's door, she popped
open the trunk and checked the contents, which she
knew by rote. Fire extinguisher, blanket, first aid
kit, teddy bear, flex cuffs, rubber gloves and a box
of double-ought buck shotgun shells. She removed
the shells and closed the trunk. She preferred to
have the extra ammo up front where she could get
to it quicker.

Once in the driver's seat, she opened the glove
compartment and put the shotgun shells inside. She
saw a small city map inside, some hand
disinfectant gel and someone's candy wrapper. She
grabbed the wrapper and tossed it in the small litter
bag next to the transmission hump.

Katie turned the key to the on position. The radio
booted up, signaled ready and displayed the word

'North' for channel one. She hit the shotgun release button and pulled the 12-gauge from the upright holder between the two seats. Stepping out of the car, she unloaded the four shells inside, cleared the weapon by checking the chamber visually, then racking it four times in quick succession. The small bandoleer on the stock held five shells. Pointing the shotgun at the empty concrete wall of the basement sally port, Katie did a tactical reload. If she were to use the gun, she would chamber one round, then immediately replace with one from the bandoleer. This gave the "street howitzer" five rounds loaded and four on the bandoleer.

As Katie stepped lightly back to the car to replace the shotgun, she saw Matt Westboard removing his from the patrol car in front of her.

"Three-ninety-seven," he said to her with a grin, pointing to his car with his free hand. He was referring to the patrol car's fleet number, Katie knew.

"So?" She replied, trying to appear disinterested, but she knew exactly what he was driving at.

"So? So, I've got the queen of the fleet here. Only eighteen hundred miles." He motioned toward Katie's car. "That one's got about a hundred and eighteen thousand on it."

Katie shrugged, trying not to smile. "Four wheels and a siren are all I need."

"How about a horse and buggy, then? Probably faster than that toilet."

"You just cost yourself a free cup of coffee." Katie leaned into her car and snapped the shotgun into place, closing the large metal clip that held it securely. Westboard was saying something that she couldn't make out, but she ignored him, testing her overhead rotator blue-and-reds, her alley lights and her overhead takedown lights. Then she turned on her spotlight and shined it right in Westboard's face. He smiled, closing his eyes and turning away. Even in the room-level light of the basement, the power of the spotlight was impressive.

Katie snapped the spotlight off after a few torturous moments, then exited her vehicle.

"Anything else you want to say about my car, Westboard?"

Westboard laid the shotgun across his front seat and pretended to be grabbing at floating balls in the air. "I'm blinded by the light," he sang.

"Doofus," Katie muttered with a grin. She opened her back door and searched her back seat thoroughly to ensure that nothing had been left in there from the previous shift. She did this, as did everyone, before and after anyone was in the seat. If someone had dumped something in the car, it could be attributed to the proper owner. Especially if the item were contraband, which was usually the case.

Her pre-flight checks complete, Katie returned to the driver's seat and adjusted the seat position and mirrors. Westboard resumed checking his own car into service. In her rear-view mirror, she could see the newest rookie, Jack Willow, checking and double-checking everything. Well, she had done the same thing while she was on probation, hadn't she? You couldn't afford to make a lot of mistakes that first year. Truth be told, you couldn't *ever* afford to make a lot of mistakes on this job. Sometimes not even one.

When she looked forward again, Westboard was pulling out of the sally port and up the ramp. She shook her head in amazement. She'd ridden with him a few times and he could check a car into service faster than anyone she knew.

Katie started the car and drove carefully out the sally port and up the ramp. When she turned onto the street, she hit her yelp siren, then the wail siren and air horn; three short bursts to verify each worked. The poor troops on Days and Swings weren't allowed to blast their siren and air horn because court was in session, but on Graveyard they were able to blast away.

Last, she checked the intercom, which she tested just by turning it on and clicking the mike. It was functional. She turned it off.

Her eyes swept the gauges on the dashboard. Everything was fine except her fuel gauge, which showed at three-eighths of a tank. She frowned. *You can't tell me the swing-shift officers are too busy to turn in the cars gassed up and ready to go.*

She keyed the mike. "Adam-116, in service."

"Adam-116, go ahead."

"Officer 407, driving vehicle 341, also."

"Copy. Go ahead your also."

"If I'm clear, I need to go signal-five for fuel."
Signal- five meant the city garage where the gas
pumps were.

*"Copy. You are clear, but I have a neighborhood
dispute holding."*

Katie sighed. "Neighborhood disputes" were the
bane of swing shift. There weren't as many on
graveyard, but they sometimes popped up early in
the shift. A Neighborhood Dispute usually meant
some old woman saying "So-and-so pulled my
flowers" or two sets of feuding parents called
because little Johnny hit little Billy and now they
want the little criminal arrested. Seldom was there
any law enforcement action that could be taken,
and it resulted in an incredible drain on an officer's
time, but it had to be endured.

Most of these people paid taxes and they wanted
police service. Since it might be the only time they
saw their police department in action unless they
were on the receiving end of a traffic citation, all
officers were *explicitly* commanded to go and
investigate thoroughly and to make everyone as
happy as possible. Often, the same call wouldn't
even be dispatched later on in the graveyard shift,
or might be dealt with in five minutes if it were.
This call was probably a swing shift holdover.

"Go ahead your dispute," Katie told radio.

*"1119 W. Prudence. Caller states neighbor
children are harassing her son. Also states the
parent of the harassing children encourages it.
1119 W. Prudence."*

"Copy. I'll be en route when I clear signal-five."

***

Karl Winter tucked his shirt into his pants and buckled his belt. The jangling sound carried in the quiet locker room. Winter had caught a late DV call that turned into a huge mess. He'd only just finished the paperwork. As he changed, he'd been watching Sgt. David Poole, who sat on the long bench that ran down the center of the aisle between the lockers. He'd been there when Winter walked in at the end of the shift. He continued to sit and stare at his open locker, completely lost in thought, the entire time Winter changed his clothes only five lockers away.

"Sarge?" Winter finally said. "You okay?"

Poole turned slowly to face him but didn't answer.

Winter's eyes narrowed with concern.

"Dave?"

"I'm fine, Karl." Poole answered in a dry, croaking voice. "Just tired. Lots of reports to read at the end of shift."

Winter knew that was a lie but decided not to push too hard. "Sorry. Mine was one of them. Listen, the guys went over to Duke's for choir practice right after shift. End of the week, you know? They're probably still there. I'm headed over as soon as I get changed. You want to come along?"

Poole shook his head wordlessly and returned to staring at his locker.

Winter stood uncomfortably for a long moment. He debated asking Poole a second time but knew the next response he got would be less than kind.

He left wordlessly, with Poole still staring darkly into his locker.

***

Katie MacLeod felt her patience slipping.

"Just what is it you want me to do, ma'am?" she asked for the third time.

The complainant, a fortyish housewife, gave Katie a look of exasperation. "Well, it's obvious, isn't it? I want those three Bailey kids arrested for harassment. Can you do that or are you just too stupid?"

A flash of anger washed over Katie and she forced herself to wait five seconds before replying.

"Ma'am, what is your name?"

"I told you before. You forget already?"

Katie removed her pocket notebook. "I meet a lot of people. I'll write it down this time."

"It's Evelyn Masters. My husband works for the County."

Good for you and your husband. Katie wrote down the woman's name.

"Now, Mrs. Masters, tell me exactly why you think the Bailey children should be arrested."

"Oh, it's not just the little brats that should go. That no-good father encourages it. He should be arrested for contributing to the juvenility of a child." Evelyn Masters gave Katie the resolute nod that is reserved for the all-knowing.

Katie took a deep breath and let it out, trying not to sigh. "You're saying that the Bailey children assaulted your oldest son, and that the father encourages this behavior."

"Yes. He doesn't work, you know. Goes out all night drinking, then comes home and sleeps all day. Must be on welfare, the lot of them." She gave another nod.

"I see. And what's your oldest child's name?"

"Brian."

"And where is Brian now?"

She gave Katie a strange look. "At a friend's house, where he's been since school let out. You think I don't send my kids to school or something?"

Katie didn't answer right away. She pretended to write in her notebook while she thought about the situation. She really wanted to strangle this obnoxious woman, but she doubted that Sgt. Shen would consider that a satisfactory resolution to this oh-so-important problem.

"Mrs. Masters, let me have a talk with the Baileys, then I'll come back and talk with you again."

"All right. But don't be surprised if you find drugs in that house. That's *if* they even let you in." She gave Katie another knowing nod.

Katie left the house and walked up the block to a small tan house. The yard appeared well-tended. A tricycle lay on its side by the front porch. Katie advised radio of her new location as she knocked on the door.

The door opened and a man in his mid-thirties wearing a pair of boxer shorts and a tattered robe stood rubbing his eyes. When he noticed Katie's uniform, his eyes widened slightly and he closed his robe self-consciously.

"Can I help you, officer?"

"Mr. Bailey?"

The man nodded.

"May I come in and talk with you for a few minutes?"

"Sure." He opened the screen door and let her into the living room. On the couch sat three kids, two boys and a girl who were now more interested in her presence than the cartoons they'd been watching. Katie smiled warmly at them as she looked around the room. It contained the normal clutter one expected in households where children lived.

"May I ask what this is all about?" Mr. Bailey asked.

Katie asked, "Which child is Tommy?"

Mr. Bailey pointed to the largest child on the end of the couch. "Why?"

"Well, according to Mrs. Masters, Tommy has been beating up on her son Brian. With your encouragement, Mr. Bailey."

"Oh, jeez." Mr. Bailey rubbed his eyes and sat in an easy chair. "That old witch is telling tales again. Look, Officer, Brian is a little terror in this neighborhood. He is the bully of the block. My kids are under strict orders to avoid him. Yesterday, he started picking on Clay, my youngest there. Tommy stood up to him and punched him in the nose when Brian wouldn't leave them alone. I saw the whole thing from the backyard."

"Did you encourage it?" Katie asked.

Mr. Bailey shifted nervously in his seat. "Well, sorta. I told him afterwards that it was a good thing that he stuck up for his brother. I mean, I know fighting is wrong and all, but you can't let the bullies rule the world, either. We had a talk about it."

Katie glanced at the three children. They sat calmly, watching her. No one asked her for stickers, which surprised her. That was the thing most kids asked for right away.

"Okay, Mr. Bailey. I figured it might be something like that."

Katie turned her attention to Tommy, who had been watching enraptured. "Tommy? Your daddy explained to you about fighting?"

Tommy nodded.

"You make sure you always listen to your Mom and Dad."

All three children nodded. When Katie turned her attention to Mr. Bailey, he smiled.

"They're good kids, really, officer. I work nights and my wife works days, so they don't get as much time with us as I'd like, but they're doing okay, you know?"

"Everything looks fine here," Katie said, turning for the door. "Continuing to avoid Brian is the best policy. I'll take care of Mrs. Masters."

"Thank you."

Katie walked back to the Master's house. Evelyn Masters waited on the front porch, her arms crossed.

"Did you arrest those little hellions?"

"No, Mrs. Masters, I didn't. They tell a completely different story."

"Well, they're just lying."

"Either way, I can't take any action without physical evidence or witnesses. And besides that, a child under the age of twelve is deemed incapable of committing a crime in the state of Washington."

"You're kidding."

Katie shook her head. She'd left out the fact that a child between eight and twelve could be found capable of committing a crime if it could be shown that the child knew the difference between right and wrong. That little factoid would remain her secret. She didn't want to give this woman anywhere to go.

"So you're just going to do nothing?"

"No, ma'am. I've given those children explicit orders not to have any contact with Brian. Of course, this order has to be reciprocal to maintain objectivity."

Mrs. Masters's eyes narrowed. "What's that mean?"

"It means that Brian can't talk with them, either."

"Why would he want to?"

"My point exactly. If that's all, then I—"

"Is there going to be a report on this?"

Katie almost sighed but caught herself. *There's no reason for a report of this,* she thought angrily. *I shouldn't even be here. And I certainly shouldn't be tied up an additional thirty minutes later in my shift working on this go-nowhere report.*

She forced herself to keep an even voice. "There is a report in the computer that I came here, ma'am. If there are any future problems, you can ask them to send the same officer. They'll have my number." *And hopefully I won't be working.*

When Mrs. Masters didn't answer right away, Katie allowed herself a small smile. "I'm sure things will be better now I have this verbal no-contact order in place. Good luck." She turned and walked back to her car.

It wasn't until she got into the car, drove out of the neighborhood and cleared One-David (officer contact - no report) that she finally allowed herself a long sigh.

What a total busybody. I need something cold to drink.

***

Karl Winter sat at the table with Ridgeway and Will Reiser. They'd arrived early and found their usual table in the corner occupied by some newcomers. Johnny apologized, but the three men didn't mind. As Ridgeway pointed out, "The beer tastes the same at any table."

Winter looked at the date on his digital watch, which Mary had bought for him two Christmases ago. He'd protested, preferring a watch with a face and two hands but Mary told him it was time to enter the latter half of the twentieth century.

The date now read August 24th, which put him at just over eight months to go. It also told him that Gio was an hour late and probably wasn't coming. All three of them knew he'd been seeing the blonde he met in here, even though he kept uncharacteristically close-mouthed about the affair. Winter had never known Gio to miss an end-of-week beer with the guys over a woman.

"Scarface has nineteen hits now, according to Major Crimes," Reiser said. "Probably three or four more that are uncertain. He got money on almost all of them."

Ridgeway didn't seem impressed. "Major Crimes can pound sand for all I care."

Winter didn't join the conversation. Ridgeway had become increasingly irritable over the past few weeks. More and more people knew about his wife's affair, thanks to her openness and the couple's common friends. Ridgeway might have been unhappy about losing her, but he was even unhappier about everyone knowing his business.

"You know what Kahn said to me?" Ridgeway asked.

"What?"

"That IA poster boy said that if I would have shot that copycat instead of smacking him, then Major Crimes would've never got an admission from him that he wasn't the real Scarface. Hart could claim to the press that all these new robberies were copycats. He'd be so happy that he'd let me take Poole's place as day shift lap dog."

"That's cold," Winter observed. He felt sorry for Ridgeway and Gio. Nabbing the copycat at Silver Lanes was still a good pinch. The guy committed a first-degree robbery and they arrested him. But just like no one calls the loser of the Super Bowl the second best team in the NFL, almost getting Scarface didn't quite cut it among the other officers. Everything on the police department was high-speed, low drag.

"You know that arrest went to Internal Affairs?"

"Why?"

"Use of force. Per the El-tee Prick himself."
Ridgeway took a hard slug of his beer and signaled
to Johnny that he wanted a shot. Then he turned to
face Winter and Reiser. "You know what their
main beef is?"

Both men shook their heads. Discussing IA
investigations, ongoing or otherwise, was strictly
forbidden. Rarely did anyone observe that rule.

Ridgeway ticked off the facts on his fingers. "That
radio didn't broadcast anything specific about a
gun. That I saw no weapon before I cracked him.
That the fake gun was under the seat. And that
using my gun as a striking instrument is forbidden
in department policy and procedures." He smiled
bitterly.

Winter shook his head in disgust.

"I can't believe that," Reiser said. *"He just
committed an armed robbery and he was reaching
inside his jacket!"*

Johnny set Ridgeway's shot in front of him.
Ridgeway threw it back and grimaced. "Imagine
that. They said I could have justified shooting him
but not pistol-whipping him."

No one spoke as Ridgeway continued.

"So let's recap. My wife throws me over for a
pansy fireman. Which everyone is now aware of
because she is out there running her mouth. Then,
instead of killing some dumb sonofabitch, I give
him a headache. IA comes to talk to me and *of*

course they have to send the Brass Bitch to do the interview. Four goddamn investigators in IA, one of them is a woman, and I get her. I just know she is going to recommend a finding of improper conduct." Ridgeway's voice rose as he spoke. "This shithead robber will probably sue, in which case the department can step aside and lay all the responsibility on me. 'Look, we gave him proper training. We never said he could hit the guy with his gun. He was operating outside the scope of his employment.' So now Shithead Copycat gets to fight over my stuff with Alice and her little fireman. Now isn't that all just absolutely, fucking *wonderful*!"

At the last word, Ridgeway slammed his palm against the table, rattling the glasses. Conversation in the bar stopped abruptly and all eyes turned to their table, including a disapproving look from Johnny. Winter held up his hand slightly and waved him off. Ridgeway stared at the table, oblivious to it all.

Winter and Reiser sat silently. In a few seconds, conversation again picked up throughout the bar. It took another few minutes for the dark cloud over the table to dissipate. Ridgeway brooded, feeding it.

Winter broke the silence, telling them about his encounter with Poole in the locker room.

"No kidding?" Reiser asked.

"No kidding. It was strange."

"What do you expect?" Ridgeway asked. "His wife pulled the same thing on him that Alice did on me.

If you throw in being Hart's lackey, he's got to feel like shit about life right now. I'm surprised he hasn't eaten his gun yet."

"Don't say things like that, Mark," Winter said, more sharply than he intended.

Ridgeway didn't react to Winter's rebuke. "I'm telling you," he said, "sometimes a guy thinks about things like that."

Winter eyed Ridgeway closely. "But not you, right?"

Ridgeway grunted and took a slug from his glass.

"Mark?"

"What?"

"Not you, right?"

Ridgeway stared at him, expressionless. "No, Mother Winter. Not me."

"Good."

A short silence followed, then Winter waved for another round. "I volunteered for Hart's task force," he said, trying to change the subject.

"No lie?" Reiser asked, joining in the conspiracy.

"Yeah. I drew the rover position, tomorrow night. I think I'll put my theory to the test."

"Theory?" asked Reiser.

Before Winter could answer, Ridgeway broke in.

"Just make sure you shoot him, Karl. Don't be merciful. Mercy is for the weak."

Reiser half-nodded. "Mark's right, in a way. Not for the IA reason, but this guy is either really smart or really crazy. Either way, don't fool around."

"It's drugs," Ridgeway said. "He's doing this to support a habit. Has to be."

Winter had already come to that conclusion. He relayed his theory about the woman accomplice in a car to the two men. Both nodded.

"Sounds reasonable. Either that or he is an Olympic-class runner," Reiser joked.

"Those druggies have no strength. They can't run," Ridgeway said. "You do have one thing on your side, though, Karl."

"What's that?"

Ridgeway grinned but there was no humor in it. "If his getaway driver is a woman, she will eventually screw him over."

Winter and Reiser chuckled, but it did little to relieve Ridgeway's dark mood.

Winter rose, dropping a twenty on the table. "Have a couple on me, gents. I'm going home before I start to believe all these evil lies about the fairer sex."

Ridgeway and Reiser raised their bottles in salute as he left Duke's.

Outside, the air remained comfortably warm but he could feel the cool promise of night. He was glad that Reiser would stay with Ridgeway a little longer. A man needed his friends at a time like this.

His Corsica started up without hesitation, and he let it idle for a minute before leaving the parking lot and driving toward home. Already, he could see Mary's bright eyes dancing. He could feel her smallness as she pressed against him for a hug. He could smell her delicious cooking, a skill hard-won over the years. He could see her apron, perhaps splashed with flour or sauce and the small wine glass on the counter that she sipped on for hours before it was empty. And he knew he would soon taste the wine that would be on her lips.

***

T-Dog reached for the phone. When Morris said now, he meant *right now*, motherfucker.

He dialed the number from memory.

Jimmy answered. "Hello?"

T-Dog smiled at Jimmy's nervous tone. That was good. It would make things easier. He waited a few moments before answering. He could almost smell Jimmy's sweat on the other end of the line.

"Hello? Hello?"

"Jimmy. It's T-Dog."

"Oh." A tiny pause hung in the air. "What's up?"

"I need your car tomorrow night."

"The brown Chevy?"

"No, the Maserati. Of course the Chevy, you idiot. Drive it over about seven."

There was another, longer pause.

"Did you hear me, bitch?"

"Uh, yeah. I kinda had something going, though."

"Reschedule."

Pause. Then, "Okay, T-Dog. You think you could hook me up when I come over? I'm hurting."

T-Dog grinned at the desperation in Jimmy's voice. "Yeah, sure. Ten for a twenty-piece, since you're giving up your car for the night."

"Thanks, man."

"Seven o'clock. Don't forget." He hung up without waiting for a response.

Dialing, again from memory, he switched gears. He punched the proper buttons and paged Cally. Had to be respectful this time. Cally was no addict. He had some juice.

It took only three minutes for the phone to ring. T-Dog picked it up.

"Cat?"

"No. T-Dog."

"Unh," Cally grunted. "'Sup?"

"I need two gatts. Before tomorrow night."

"Baby nines?"

"That's fine, unless you got anything bigger?"

"Not here. I got the baby nines right now, but anything bigger might take a while. More than a day."

T-Dog considered. Three-eighties were small pistols, good for concealment, but they lacked a lot in the power department.

"I guess I'll take the babies. Are the numbers filed off?"

"They can be."

"Need 'em that way."

They haggled briefly over price and T-Dog hung up. He turned to Morris, who lounged on the sofa, drinking from a forty-ounce bottle of beer.

"Got the drive and the gatts."

Morris nodded his approval and licked his top lip. "Thas' right. Gonna get that lily-ass motherfucker."

***

Breakfast usually began around five in the morning. Units started asking if they were clear for a seven, and it was a rare morning when every unit that asked was not cleared. Cops were notoriously poor tippers, but they were generally loyal with their dining business. Too many cooks and dishwashers were arrested to risk going someplace they didn't know, unless they wanted to risk someone spitting in the food. Or worse.

Mary's Café was located at Birch and Rowan, both arterial streets. Long established as an officer-friendly restaurant, police cars crowded the small parking lot every morning. Baker sector officers crossed division and drove almost twenty blocks into Adam Sector to take breakfast there. If Hart had been the graveyard lieutenant, this never would have happened, but Saylor allowed it. The only stipulations were unspoken: a couple of units remained in service to shag the occasional call and units cleared to respond to anything that needed a response. The north-side troops happily adhered to these requirements.

Katie MacLeod didn't care much for breakfast food. Sometimes, though, it felt good to get out of the car and do reports on a nice table with something hot to drink. Besides, there were two schools of thought on doing reports in the car. One held that it was good because you stayed in service and could answer calls quickly. The other held that it was dangerous because you were vulnerable while writing, or that you couldn't accomplish much writing if you maintained the proper level of alertness.

Katie belonged to the first school, countering the danger factor by backing into a location where she could only be approached from the front or parking in the center of a large, empty parking lot. That way any movement attracted her attention.

Still, the coffee here at Mary's tasted good and there was company, if you wanted it. She didn't, and signaled that to the others by sitting alone a booth away from the group already present. Besides, she wanted the solitude for other reasons.

Or reason.

Oh, hell, it was Stef.

She'd avoided him since that morning. Confusion flooded her senses whenever she thought of the situation. She paused while writing a burglary report.

Why do I keep coming back to this?

Because she liked him, she knew. He'd been a nice guy and there were some sparks between them, ever since the Academy.

But she was on the rebound. And he… well, who knew where he was on this?

Katie bit her lip. He hadn't tried too hard to go out of his way to talk to her since that night. Yeah, maybe she'd avoided him a little, but she got the sense that he'd been avoiding her, too.

Maybe that was best. Love on the rebound. Dipping your pen in company ink. Cops working together and sleeping together. None of it sounded smart to her.

She wondered if dating another cop would make it easier to deal with the stress of the job. After all, you wouldn't have to describe it to the other person. They'd understand it perfectly. Then again, what if the stress wasn't relieved but instead doubled? And what about when he became protective, coming on all her calls, worrying about her all the time? Eventually that would happen, she knew. She hesitated, not wanting to acknowledge the next obvious question: What if they broke up? Working around an ex-lover would suck.

Jesus, Katie thought. *Why am I worried about this? He's obviously not. We had our little fling and it's over with. There's nothing else to it.*

Right?

Katie shut off debate and dug into her report.

***

Gio lay in the early morning darkness. The red numbers of his clock gave him another thirty minutes of sleep, but Gio wasn't tired.

He could still feel Marilyn's presence in his bed. She'd risen at midnight and left. She seemed regretful, but she had to work in the morning and could not wear the same clothes two days in a row. Gio watched her dress in the darkness, admiring the silhouette of her body and head standing and bending like a dance. Her lips radiated warmth when she kissed him wetly and slipped out.

Now, he watched the minutes slip by on his clock and dreamt a waking dream of her. He realized Marilyn was different for him. That difference frightened him.

He couldn't be falling in love with her.

Could he?

Was this what it was like?

He never expected to feel this way. Never really thought it possible. Now, he felt a pang in his stomach whenever he thought of her.

And what was he afraid of?

Gio took a deep breath and let it out. He knew what he feared. He'd never really cared how the woman felt, as long as she felt like sleeping with him. Now, he found himself worrying about how Marilyn felt. Obsessing about it.

She had to feel the same way. Or at least be starting to. How could she make love to him like she did and not? She had to feel it. She had to know he did, too.

But what if she didn't sense his feelings?

And what if she didn't feel the same way?

What if she got tired of him? Or doubted him?

Lying in the darkness, watching the crimson bars turn minute by minute, Gio decided he would tell her.

***

Just where everyone wants to be, Kopriva thought. *Standing tall in the Lieutenant's office.*

He stood rigidly in front of Lt. Saylor's desk as the shift commander read the complaint to him. He recognized the complainant long before he was told her name.

Saylor finished reading and raised his head to look at Kopriva. "Now, Officer Kopriva, I have to advise you that you have the right to have a Guild representative here with you during this proceeding."

Damn. That meant he was going to get hammered. Well, if it stayed at shift level, that was better than seeing it go to IA.

"I waive that right, sir," he told Saylor.

"Sign here, then."

He handed Kopriva the pen and the officer scrawled his name.

"Now, tell me. Does Ms. Wilson have a valid complaint?"

Kopriva considered. Saylor was a straight shooter. He would give him a fair shake, he decided.

"I don't know, sir. She definitely blew the stoplight. I wasn't too concerned in listening to how she thought the light was yellow. I suppose I was a little short with her. But I never said anything unprofessional."

"Do you know where she was headed when you stopped her?"

Kopriva shook his head.

"Her son's birthday party. Probably his last. He has terminal cancer."

"Oh." Kopriva suddenly felt like a heel.

Saylor didn't say anything for a long moment. Then he wrote something at the bottom of the complaint sheet. Without looking up, he said, "This will be considered a verbal counseling, as noted on the complaint form. Your actions were not improper." His gaze locked on Kopriva. "You couldn't have known, Stef, but maybe next time, listen a little?"

"Yes, sir."

Saylor slid the paper across the desk to him. "Just sign that I counseled you, okay?"

Kopriva signed and returned the pen.

"We all get a little frustrated sometimes, right? Just take it out on the right people." He gave Kopriva a wink. "And you did *not* hear that last part from me."

"Thanks, Lieutenant."

Saylor nodded and glanced at the wall clock. Thirty minutes of the shift remained. "Why don't you call it a night?"

Kopriva thanked him again and left the office. He changed quickly and hurried to his car. As he pulled out of the lot, he saw Katie parking her patrol car and securing it. He kept driving and did not meet her eye.

218

Saturday, August 24th
Graveyard Shift

Katie MacLeod drove slowly down the side street, gazing at the houses she passed. She imagined the people who might live inside. Their stories. Their problems.

She smiled bitterly about that last thought. What did most of them know about problems? Oh sure, they had romantic problems, some of them. Things like her current situation. Getting dumped. Sleeping with someone you shouldn't. Nothing unique about that.

But she was willing to bet no one in the houses she cruised past ever had to decide whether to shoot someone or not. They just trundled along in their little lives, working, watching TV and going to the mall and left those questions for the police to answer.

Katie sighed. She needed a vacation. A vacation from her life.

"Adam-116, Adam-114."

Katie keyed her mike and listened as Matt Westboard did the same.

"A domestic at 5117 N. Celtic Avenue. Caller can hear yelling and banging. Nothing further. No listing on occupants of the house."

Katie copied and gave her location, about two minutes away from the address. Westboard copied from nearly downtown. Radio repeated their locations. Katie cursed at the dispatcher. Wasn't there someone closer than Westboard to back her?

Light traffic allowed her to make good time, and she arrived on scene in less than a minute and a half. She checked out, parked a half a block away and walked in. The yards in this neighborhood seemed well tended and all the houses looked nice. Of course, that didn't mean anything. DV's happened in mansions and shacks alike.

She approached the house carefully. Except for the muffled sound of a television, no sound came from inside. The shades were drawn. Katie kept her radio covered with her hand as she crept along the side of the house. Still nothing.

The open porch had steps on both sides. She stepped up slowly, listening.

Then came the screaming, muffled through the closed windows and door. At least one male and one female. She could hear slaps and the sound of furniture being struck. It went on for about five seconds, then subsided for a moment.

Katie eased the screen door open and locked it out, her heart pounding. Clear as day, she heard another roar of human voices and sounds of struggle. Then a female voice cried, "Oh, no!" followed by a booming male voice, "Get up you worthless piece of shit!" More sounds of strikes and furniture.

Katie keyed her mike and spoke in a subdued voice. "-16, how far off is -14?"

"Division and Buckeye."

Damn. Katie's breathing was shallow and rapid. She forced herself to inhale and then exhale more deeply.

More screaming. Loud pounding.

Another deep breath. Sweat collected on her upper lip and trickled from her armpits. Her vest seemed extra heavy.

She had to go in.

Damn!

"Adam-116, it sounds violent. Have -14 step it up." She swallowed thickly and licked her lips. "I'm going in."

Radio copied. The dispatcher relayed her message and restricted the channel, her voice tense. Katie didn't notice. She wiped her damp palms on her uniform pants and drew her pistol. She checked the doorknob.

Locked.

Another female screamed, "Oh, no, not again!"

Immediately after, a male yelled, "Get out of there!"

Katie stepped back and booted the door, putting her weight forward and striking just to the side of the knob, as she had been taught. A loud crack and the door swung partially open. A small jagged piece of wood held it weakly to the doorjamb. Katie put her shoulder into the door and came crashing into the house.

As soon as she made entry, she swept her gun across all open spaces. She saw the threat immediately. A white male stood in the center of the living room off to her right with a fireplace poker in his right hand. He held it raised as if to strike. On the couch in front of him cringed a white female. Both stared at her in surprise.

"Police! Drop that poker now!"

The man just stood there, staring.

"Do it!" Katie's finger slipped into the trigger guard. She began to squeeze.

The man did not move.

"If you don't drop that poker right now, I will shoot you," she told him in a low, intense voice.

The man shook his head as if just waking up. The poker clattered to the floor and he raised his hands.

"Now turn away from me."

The man complied.

"Down on your knees."

The man dropped to his knees. "What's going on?"

Katie ignored his question and kept her gun trained on the center of his back. "Clasp your hands behind your head. Cross your ankles."

The man did both without hesitation. She saw him trembling even from across the room.

Katie eased around the couch, not taking her eyes off the suspect. "Are you all right, ma'am?"

"W-what?"

"Do you need medical treatment?"

"No. W-what's all this about?"

Katie allowed herself to take a quick glance at the woman, who sat on the couch, a bottle of beer still clutched in her hand. She had no visible injuries. Katie noticed that her makeup wasn't even smeared.

"You aren't injured?"

"No. Why would I be?"

A terrible feeling seeped into Katie. "Did he hit you?"

Her question was met with a confused look. "Fred? No."

"But I heard yelling and—"

"Boom-Boom," Fred said, turning back to look over his shoulder.

"What?"

"We… we were watching Boom-Boom. The middle-weight boxer from River City?"

Katie glanced at the television and noticed the small ESPN logo in the lower left corner. Two men were boxing.

"You never heard of Boom-Boom Bassen? He's number fourteen in the world."

"No," Katie whispered.

"He got knocked down," the woman explained. "The black guy knocked him down."

"Can I sit down now?" the man asked.

"What about the poker? Why'd he have that?" Katie asked the woman.

"Someone was breaking in," she answered, gesturing toward the door.

Katie motioned to Fred. "Go sit down."

Katie moved the poker and holstered her gun. *Boxing fans. The only thing worse were football fans.*

She keyed her mike. "Adam-116, code four."

"Copy, code four. Adam-114 and all other units may disregard."

Katie turned back to the couple who still stared at her, a shocked look on their faces. "We received a 911 call," she explained. "Someone reported a disturbance."

Outside, a car approached and then a door slammed.

Fred raised his hand tentatively, as if he were in school. Katie nodded at him. "Uh, who's gonna fix our door?"

"The city will pay for it. Would you like to speak to a supervisor, sir?"

Matt Westboard appeared in the doorway. His eyes surveyed the scene, then came to rest on Katie. He raised a single eyebrow questioningly, just like Mr. Spock.

"Boom-Boom Bassen," she told him.

"Number fourteen in the world," Fred added.

***

Lt. Hart stood in front of the lectern. He'd completed his briefing for the robbery special detail, repeating himself several times to ensure his instructions were clear. Plainclothes observers were not to engage the robber alone. He didn't want anyone hot-dogging this operation.

"Any questions?"

No response. He looked at the seven participants. Were they here to catch the robber or just to suck up overtime? Probably some of both, he decided, but for the first time since he made lieutenant, he didn't care what the OT costs were. He wanted Scarface.

That was his ticket to Captain's bars.

***

Gio sat across the table from Marilyn. The dinner had been delicious. He didn't care for seafood, but Marilyn loved it. He ordered a steak, though, so it all worked out.

He stared at her, watching her eat daintily, dab her lips with a napkin, sip her wine.

Just tell her.

She caught his gaze and smiled slowly. "What?"

God, she's beautiful.

"Marilyn?"

"Gio?" she said, slightly teasing.

He swallowed. He'd said these words before, long ago, as a tool to get what he wanted. Later, he learned not to resort to such desperate tactics. But now, when he might mean them, the words stuck in his throat.

"Gio? What?" She seemed amused at his shyness.

Maybe she knew.

He took a deep breath. "I..." he paused and looked directly into her eyes. "I..."

Marilyn looked at him, confused. Then realization flooded her eyes and her face fell.

Gio changed tactics quickly, but the damage had been done. "I... really thought the steak was good here," he finished lamely. "How was your shrimp?"

A long pause spun out while she set her fork down and dabbed at her lips with her napkin. Only a few moments ago, he'd found that act beautiful. Now it seemed ominous.

"Gio, I..." she stopped. He looked for tears but saw none. He felt dread creep in. "I like you. I like you a lot. We've had fun, some good times..." she gave a small smile. "...great sex. But I'm not really interested in anything serious. I mean, were you?"

Gio looked away. He couldn't answer, couldn't look at her.

"I asked the bartender about you and he said..." she trailed off. "Were you looking for something serious, Gio?"

He shrugged. "Maybe. I don't know. I haven't dated anyone else since we met."

She didn't answer. He looked up, and her silence told him that the same was not true for her.

He'd made a terrible mistake.

"Maybe we should stop seeing each other," Marilyn said quietly.

He stared at her as if he didn't understand. But he did. He knew the dance of the breaking hearts. He just usually led.

"Maybe I should go," she added with quiet finality.

"Maybe," Gio whispered.

She paused for a moment, her mouth open as if to speak. He knew the words that hesitated behind her lips. *I'm sorry.* Instead, she stood and walked away from the table without a word.

***

Katie leaned against her car, wishing that she smoked. A cigarette would have been a nice distraction. Westboard stood next to her, hands in his back pockets, rocking on his heels. Both were waiting for Sergeant Shen to finish inside the house.

"Maybe I should join the fire department," Katie muttered. "Sleep my whole shift."

Westboard grinned and shook his head. "You didn't do anything wrong, Katie."

"I blew the call," she replied.

"Depends on how you look at it."

Katie turned to look at him. "What is *that* supposed to mean?"

Westboard continued to rock lightly on his heels. "Well, it depends on if you want to take the long or the short view."

"The what?" Katie shook her head. "You've lost me."

Westboard removed his hands from his pockets and rubbed them together. "It's simple. If you take the short view, then the outlook is that you misjudged a call and broke down a door you didn't need to. What's the downside of that? The city pays for a door and maybe a citizen is a little pissed off. Or not, depending on how well Shen is doing in there." He thumbed at the house.

"The short view sounds like exactly what happened," Katie said.

"It is," Westboard answered, "but in the greater scheme of your career, how big a deal is it? Not much of one. That's where the long view comes in. The long view says you were faced with a dangerous situation. You were alone. You had to decide whether your personal safety was more important than that woman's safety inside the house."

"She wasn't in any danger," Katie argued quietly.

"You didn't know that. Had every reason to believe she was in very real danger. You were faced with a choice and made a decision, which tells you a bit about who you are, doesn't it? Maybe answers a question or two about yourself?"

Katie didn't answer.

"You went in and did what was necessary," Westboard continued. "I'd say the long view is that you'll always do what it takes."

Slowly, Katie nodded. He made sense. "When did you get so wise?"

Westboard shrugged. "Everyone has their demons, Katie. You faced yours."

"And what are yours?" Katie asked playfully.

Westboard blanched and looked away.

Before she could apologize, the screen door squeaked open and Sgt. Shen appeared in the doorway. The lithe supervisor gave a wave to Fred as he walked down the walkway toward Katie and Westboard.

"Well," he said when he reached them, "that's taken care of."

"Are they filing a complaint?" Katie asked.

"Complaint? No." Shen smiled. "I assured them the City would pay for a new door and cover the cost of any dry cleaning for soiled undergarments."

Katie gave a sigh of relief. "I'm sorry, Sarge. I—"

Shen raised a hand. "You already explained. Your actions were reasonable. Actually, they were brave and a little risky. Just write an informational report for me, okay?"

She nodded. "Thanks."

Shen smiled, then headed back to his own car.

"Hey, Sarge?" Katie called after him.

Shen turned.

"Who won the fight?"

Shen smiled. "I believe the hometown hero went down in the ninth. Left hook." He pantomimed a sharp punch to the head, then turned and continued to his car.

Katie looked at Westboard and shrugged. "Guess he's not number fourteen any more."

***

Winter pulled into the alley and shut off the engine, now centrally located for three of the five stores. The other rover would be responsible for the remaining two. Hart wanted them to drive between the stores constantly, which Winter thought was ridiculous and refused to do. The surveillance vehicle's job was to watch the store. He'd respond and watch for the getaway.

Besides, the odds that Scarface would hit tonight were not great, and the odds of hitting one of the targeted stores even slimmer. Karl Winter settled in for a long night.

He opened his lunch cooler. On top of the neatly packed sandwich, crackers and juice, Mary had placed a small note and his favorite candy bar.

Be safe and save some energy. Love, M.

He read the note with a smile, then absently placed it in his breast pocket. He closed the lunch cooler and opted for the thermos of coffee.

An hour flew by. Winter turned the ignition key to start and listened to the stereo on low volume. Like Chisolm, he had served in Vietnam, though his tour was considerably less glamorous. Just your run of the mill blood and guts and none of that Special Operations stuff. He still liked the music from that era. Whenever he heard those songs, he remembered the good times he had. The partying he did on leave. The card games in the barracks. The bad times, the scary times, remained buried. He wondered if the same were true for Tom and realized they'd never talked about it.

Winter thought about the note in his pocket and pulled it out, re-reading it. He felt like he was the only guy in the platoon with a successful relationship with a woman, except maybe for Reiser. Ridgeway's situation amounted to an ongoing soap opera. Gio flitted from woman to woman without remorse. Poole seemed to be growing more despondent and bitter every day. And then there was Mary and him.

Some guys have all the luck, Winter mused, putting the note away.

A large white Chrysler drove by. He didn't notice anything remarkable about it. An anxious white female drove and as she darted past the alley, she was looking into the back seat. Winter sipped his coffee and reached for his notebook. Best to write down the plate, just in case.

The alarm tone startled him and he spilled his coffee all over his notebook.

***

Stefan Kopriva accepted the license from the driver's hand and scrutinized it. The robbery alarm tone blared over his portable. He tossed the license back to the teenager. "Watch your speed," he ordered and hustled back to his car. Once inside, he flipped his siren on and squealed his tires as he left.

***

Hart picked up the phone half-way through the first ring. He'd heard the alarm tone.

"Is it Scarface?" he asked Carrie Anne, the radio supervisor.

"The description matches."

"I didn't hear the codeword."

"There was no 'Red Dog' given. This location was not under surveillance."

Hart swore silently and hung up the phone.

***

Winter turned on his overhead lights and put out his location. The white Chrysler pulled to the side of the road at Jackson and Cincinnati. Winter turned on every light the patrol car was equipped with, unfamiliar with their operation after so long on day shift.

Once he had showered the Chrysler in artificial light, he exited the car and approached cautiously, his right hand resting on his pistol. He considered waiting for a back-up, but didn't want to waste too much time if this were not the vehicle. His theory could be wrong, after all.

He reached the rear bumper and shined his mag light into the back seat.

***

Probationary Officer Maurice Payne drove westbound on Foothills from Crestline. He wondered how angry he'd made Bates when he caused the FTO to spill his drink on his leg. That concern faded as he struggled to place Charlie-251's location in relation to his own.

Jackson and Cincinnati.

Jackson, Jackson.

He drew a blank.

Cincinnati, then. Cincinnati was just west of Hamilton. Well, one or two west, anyway, but Hamilton curved around into Utah just north of the street he was on. So if he made a turn onto that arterial and headed along it, he would cross Jackson. Then Cincinnati would only be a block or two off.

But which way? Was Jackson north or south of this street?

Payne gripped the steering wheel, white knuckled, deathly afraid to reach for his street locator and reveal to his FTO that he didn't know.

***

Back on the telephone with dispatch, Hart barked orders at Carrie Anne. "Set up a perimeter on that store, three blocks in each direction." He squeezed the phone receiver tightly in his hands. He could not afford for Scarface to get away during his task force special. "Does Winter have a backup on the way?"

"Yes," Carrie Anne said. He heard her typing at her keyboard. "It's Baker-133, Bates and Payne."

"Where are they coming? from?"

"Crestline and Foothills as of thirty seconds ago."

"All right. Get a status check on Winter."

***

Winter shined his light throughout the interior of the car. It was dirty, but empty. No blankets, no room for anyone to hide. He checked the front seat as well. A few empty beer cans, but otherwise empty. The female driver sat with her hands firmly on the wheel, staring straight ahead.

"Charlie-251, status check."

Winter keyed his mike. "Code four."

***

"Code four."

Kopriva heard that and automatically diverted to the store to take a perimeter position. He wondered how long the delay was on this one.

***

Thirty seconds from the store, Thomas Chisolm wondered the same thing. He heard the K-9 switch from the south-side channel and respond. The victim store was short north, so the K-9 should get a fresh track.

Not that it would matter.

***

Payne clenched his jaw as he approached Hamilton. *Right or left? North or south?*

He tried to remember a call or a stop he'd had on Jackson but couldn't.

Where the hell is Jackson?

He had a fifty-fifty chance. Besides, he'd been on five perimeters before and they never caught the guy. They'd never been on time.

***

Kopriva pulled up to a stop at Mission and Standard with his overheads on, blocking traffic. He notified radio of his perimeter location. He saw another car doing the same at Hamilton and Mission and heard Thomas Chisolm check out there. Another patrol car slipped by Chisolm's location, its lights on.

Probably K-94, on his way to another fruitless track.

Kopriva wondered if the K-9 guys were getting frustrated yet.

***

Winter held the driver's license in his hand, about to go back to his car and check her name, when he paused. The driver stared straight ahead, gripping the steering wheel. She looked thin, too thin, and very nervous. Winter glanced at her driver's license. The picture was two, almost three years old and a much fuller faced smiled out from the photo.

She looked like a junkie to him. Actually, more like a crack-head. Junkies were usually tight and wouldn't talk, but crack-heads weren't so loyal.

Winter decided to interview her.

***

The throaty idle of the engine made it hard to hear the muffled voices, but he could make out most of it. He wondered why Carla stopped so soon after they left the store, but then he'd heard the tinny crackle of a police radio outside her door. There was no mistaking the calm authority in the voice he heard.

"Step out of the car, miss."

James Mace made his decision in an instant.

***

Carla sat stock-still in the front seat of the white Chrysler, just like she had been told to. *Do not get out of the car*, he had drilled into her. *Just sit there, no matter what they say. If they want you to get out of the car, we are fucked. So sit still and don't worry.*

Carla sat still, but she couldn't stop from worrying.

***

Winter waited a few moments when the driver did not immediately obey his command. Sometimes nervous people were slow. Maybe she had a warrant, too. He probably should have run her name first.

"Miss, step out of the vehicle," he ordered again.

In the next instant, he saw a flash of movement in the back seat. Winter's mind struggled to process the information. The back seat had been empty.

Winter turned, ripping his gun from his holster, but he wasn't nearly fast enough.

***

From inside the trunk, Mace pushed the back seat forward. The cushion slid across the seat and struck the back of the front seat. Carla gave a small yelp. He ignored her as he slid out of the trunk and into the back seat. Mace trained his weapon on the fat cop standing at the window. He wished for an M-16 like when he had been a Ranger, but the thirty-eight bucked slightly in his hands as he squeezed off three quick rounds. The roar of the gun filled the car.

The rear driver's side window shattered. The bullets bit into the cop and shock registered on his jowly face. Mace saw a squirt of blood leap out of the cop's left eye as his first shot went high. The other two slapped into his chest, disappearing into the dark uniform shirt.

Nice tight group.

The cop fell, disappearing from view. Carla screamed.

"Drive, you stupid bitch!" Mace screamed at her, "or I'll fucking shoot you next."

***

Winter felt himself go *thunk* on the asphalt. For a second, he couldn't see. He felt wetness on his face, the left side, but the greater pain was lower. In the chest.

He'd been hit.

He heard the squeal of tires and the thick odor of exhaust assaulted his senses.

His left hand fumbled at his belt, searching for his portable radio. He located it and slid his thumb awkwardly into the small notch at the back where he hit the tiny red panic button.

Now wait for the sirens. They're coming.

But instead, he remembered a time when he waited in the midst of sing-song Vietnamese screams and the splatting sound of AK-47's, listening for the sweet sound of helicopter rotors.

***

Another alarm tone, wondered Kopriva. *What the hell?*

"Signal-98, panic button. Charlie-251, Officer Winter. Jackson and Cincinnati. Repeat, Signal-98."

"Holy shit!" Kopriva yelled, dropping his car into gear. He punched the accelerator and flew up Standard toward Jackson. On the way, he blew past a white Chrysler, which dutifully pulled to the side to let him pass even though it drove southbound.

***

The alarm tone surprised Payne as well. He reached Hamilton.

North or south?

He decided on north, since more of the sector lay to the north of his location.

Good choice, good reason, he told himself as he

swung the police car north on Hamilton.

"What the hell are you doing?" screamed Bates.

Payne winced. Fifty-fifty shot and he lost. He turned the car around as soon as they passed the concrete island.

"Sorry," he told Bates.

"Drive faster or I will stop this car and drive myself," Bates told him, his voice steeped in cold anger.

***

As soon as he heard the garage door close, Mace pushed the cushion forward and slid out of the trunk into the back seat. He replaced the cushion again. Carla cried hard, bordering on hysterical. He slapped her without thinking twice about it.

"Shut up. Let's get upstairs." He put his jacket, the wig, gun and money into an empty gym bag. They left the small garage and made their way up the stairs to his apartment.

Carla sniffled and hitched, but otherwise maintained herself all the way up the stairs. As soon as the door closed behind her, she started to cry hysterically again. "You shot a cop!" she screamed. "Oh my God, you shot a cop."

Andrea and Leslie sat on the couch, watching her dispassionately. She turned to them both. "He shot a cop! We're all going to hang. They hang people in this state, you know."

"It'll be all right," Mace said. "No one saw us. No one knows but him, and he's as good as dead."

He wondered if that were true. He needed to turn on the TV and see what the news reported.

"Oh, God," Carla sobbed. "He shot a cop."

"Fuck that cop!" Mace snarled. "That's what he had coming."

Carla whimpered.

"The cop was the enemy," Mace said, his voice low and intense. His body felt electric. "He would have killed us if he had the chance. I did what I had to do."

Silence filled the room, except for Carla's sobbing and muttering. Mace put his gym bag on the kitchen table and turned to look at Andrea and Leslie. Andrea remained silent.

Leslie finally spoke. "Did you score any smack, baby?"

***

Karl Winter clutched at his wounds. His chest seemed constricted and pain pulsed where the bullets had hit.

Thoughts flitted through his mind.

One bullet there or two?

Jesus, that was close to his heart, wasn't it?

He should've worn his vest.

He couldn't see out of one eye.

Winter chuckled, a wet raspy sound. He had been right about Scarface, hadn't he? Almost right.

Then the pain hit again, followed by a coldness.

Mary. Mary. Had he kissed her goodbye tonight? He'd kissed her goodbye every day for twenty-four years, but he could not remember if he'd kissed her tonight.

Mary. He could hear her sweet laugh as he struggled to play the guitar. The music rang in his ears.

"The screen door slams, Mary's dress waves."

Winter's bloody hand twitched as his fingers struggled to form the chords. He tried to sing, but only a wheeze escaped his mouth.

Mary. Her soft touch on his shoulder.

Had he kissed her goodbye?

His feet were so cold.

A siren broke through his thoughts, followed by the screech of tires.

***

Kopriva leapt from the car and ran to the fallen officer. He recognized Winter more by his belly than his bloody face.

"Baker-123, officer down! Start medics, now!"

"Copy. Injuries?"

"Multiple gunshot wounds," Kopriva said, guessing.

He knelt beside Winter. Blood, coming from his left eye, covered the left side of the officer's face. That wound appeared to be only a trickle. Kopriva saw the bullet holes in his chest and heard the raspy rattle of a sucking chest wound. He applied pressure, noticing that Winter didn't have on a vest. Frantically, he struggled to recall the proper first aid.

Winter tried to mouth something to him. He leaned forward but no sound came from the veteran's lips. Winter spoke the same silent few words over and over, but Kopriva couldn't make them out. He lifted his head again. Winter continued to mouth the phrase, looking like a fish gasping for water in the bottom of a fishing boat.

Then Kopriva noticed the puddle of blood that emerged from both sides of Winter, spreading slowly outward like a pair of black wings.

He took Winter's hand and held it tightly in his.

***

Karl Winter saw the shadowy shape of a man above him but not well enough to recognize who it was. He saw the silver badge on the man's chest, though. That was what mattered. He'd been able to give his message to the man, who would give it to Mary. He didn't want her to worry at his bedside while he recovered.

The light shining from the streetlight had dimmed. He was cold, so cold.

He could barely feel the officer's grip on his hand and wished he could hold it tighter.

Had he kissed Mary goodbye?

***

"You're going to be okay, man. Just hold on." Kopriva squeezed Winter's hand tightly. He didn't know if the wounded officer could hear him or not. "Just hold on."

Hurry up with the goddamn medics!

He looked around frantically, willing them to appear. He saw fresh rubber marks beside Winter in the flashing red and blue lights. They led westbound. He realized that he'd probably passed the suspect car on his way and cursed silently.

When he looked down again, Karl Winter's eyes had frozen into a fixed stare.

Tuesday, August 27th
Day Shift

A warm August rain fell on the mourners. It began as large, fat drops, splattering noisily when they struck. A brisk wind swept in and broke up the drops, thinning them out. Within minutes, it changed into a misty sheet, lightly soaking the attending mourners.

Police Chaplain Timothy Marshall stood in the downpour, oblivious to its assault. His usually jovial face turned somber for the occasion. His only reaction to the weather was to close his eyes as he spoke words he knew by rote.

"Ashes to ashes," he intoned, his words torn and fragmented in the wetness. "Dust to dust."

Three hundred officers stood in the large cemetery, all in dress uniform or dark suits. Those closest to the chaplain heard his words and found in them no solace. Those too far away to hear shifted uncomfortably in the rain.

Lt. Alan Hart stood rigidly, unsure of his proper role. Winter had not cared for him. Neither had his friends. His sympathies would likely be rebuffed, but his distance would only serve to reinforce their image of him.

At his side, Sgt. David Poole watched Mary Winter. He knew how much Karl and she loved each other. He had often compared Sherrie to Mary until he realized he did not love his wife. He found himself envying Karl his heroic death, fearing his own would not be so glorious. A deep sadness came with the belief (*or was it knowledge,* he thought morbidly) that he would die alone and unloved.

Anthony Giovanni and Mark Ridgeway stood on each side of Mary. Neither could have known that they shared the same thoughts. Both were deeply hurt over the loss of a woman and both cursed themselves for not being with Winter when he'd needed them. He had always been there for each of them.

A furious, guilt-racked Kopriva stood in the second row of the mourning group. He felt as if he, too, had failed Winter. All the way to the hospital, he watched the paramedics work feverishly on an already dead Winter. He recognized the first few procedures as field techniques he could have performed. That knowledge slammed into his chest with a vengeance. He could have saved Winter if he had acted more quickly. All the doctor's assurances to the contrary didn't change that. The surgeons might have been able to repair a nicked aorta if he'd only given them the chance. Instead, he'd stood by while Karl Winter's life bled out onto the warm, summer asphalt.

Kopriva spotted Katie McLeod standing on the fringes of the crowd. She wore a black, calf-length dress. Simple and elegant. She looked beautiful, like a sculpture. *Beautiful and untouchable,* he reminded himself.

Standing with the pallbearers, Thomas Chisolm kept his face calm and impassive. He barely noticed the rain as it washed over him. He had attended dozens of funerals in his life, most of them after returning from Vietnam. His trip to Arlington cemetery and then, years later, to the Vietnam Memorial had been emotional ones. He'd wept openly, shamelessly, mourning for dozens, even scores, of men. Karl Winter was one man, however, and Chisolm would do him the honor of a stoic burial.

The honor guard from the local National Guard unit folded the flag in crisp motions. Their presence, along with the police motorcycle escort to the cemetery, was an honor accorded to Winter out of respect for his status as both a veteran and a policeman. The bugler stood ready at a distance.

Chisolm watched the honor guard sergeant present the flag to Mary Winter. The uniformed man spoke softly to her before returning to his squad.

Chaplain Tim gave a nod and the groundskeeper began to turn the lever. The brown casket slowly sank into the wet ground.

Mary Winter sat at the grave-side, watching them lower her husband into the earth. The solemn notes of *Taps* pierced the stillness. Her brother Aaron's strong hands rested on both her shoulders. The casket lowered out of sight as the final notes of *Taps* welled up like a tear and trailed off.

The crowd began to break up. Mary heard the murmuring of sympathies and nodded automatically, without understanding the words or seeing the faces. She knew Mark and Gio would stand with her until she was ready to leave, and that Aaron would be there to lean on throughout the day and for the weeks to come.

But it didn't matter.

Nothing could change the pain. Not the honor or respect they paid to her husband, not the insurance policy, not the hat-passing that would take place at the reception following this and not the flag she clutched to her breast.

Mary Winter began to weep and her huge, racking sobs pierced the downpour where the chaplain's words had failed.

Sunday, September 1st
Graveyard Shift

T-Dog checked that both pistols were loaded with full magazines and a round in the chamber. Everything had to be perfect. Morris was getting very touchy lately, as their nightly searches came up empty. He assured Morris that it was only a matter of time before luck would take a hand and they'd find the cop. He'd been rewarded with a ten-minute tirade. Now, he remained silent while Morris groused.

"Gonna get that cracker bitch motherfucker," Morris muttered as he sipped from his forty-ouncer. "To-*night!*"

T-Dog didn't respond, but handed him the small black .380. Morris shook his head. "Gimme the other one, dumb motherfucker." He reached out as T-Dog handed him the one with the brown grips. "The poker gun, too."

T-Dog handed him the small, two-shot derringer, which Morris liked to carry at card games.

Morris snatched it from his hand. "Stupid fuckin' Wonder Bread," he said. He shook his head at T-Dog and slipped the guns into his pockets.

T-Dog swallowed the insult dutifully, raging at it inside. Man, he was a brother. He hung with the bangers. He kept their secrets, he did their dirty work. What did it take to be accepted?

Stroking the smooth metal of the pistol's slide, T-

Dog found his answer.

***

Woodenly, Stefan Kopriva patrolled his sector. Five days had passed since Karl Winter's funeral, and the impact of the shooting on the department had not subsided. His death had not officially been pinned on Scarface, though every officer in town remained convinced it had been the elusive robber who shot Winter.

Kopriva reviewed the facts that were finally given to patrol at that evening's roll call. The license plate of the car Winter stopped came back to a 1972 Ford Maverick, but the tire marks at the scene suggested a much wider mid-to-early seventies car, like a Caprice or something similar. So, either Winter put out the wrong plate when he made the stop or more likely the plates had been switched. No shell casings were found at the scene. One of the bullets that struck Winter had been recovered. Forensics stated it was a .38 caliber, the weapon formerly used by every cop in America.

The only other clue was a driver's license at the scene belonging to Carla Dunham. River City PD showed no record of her locally, and her Department of Licensing address was in Seattle. Her picture circulated at the roll call tables.

Business continued as usual. The calls just kept coming. Burglaries, DV's, accidents, drunks. People constantly asking about the shooting. *Did you know the cop who got shot?*

Scarface had been busy, too. Three more robberies since the night of the shooting. Strangely, he had not hit on the night of the funeral, something Kopriva didn't know what to make of, if anything.

He remembered Katie at the funeral and her sculpted beauty. She hadn't cried, remaining strong in the presence of her brethren police officers. She'd caught his eye and held it for a long time while the bugler's notes floated over them. He hadn't been able to read her face.

He should have spoken with her. Hell, he wanted to. He'd wanted to be with someone very badly that night. To make love frantically with someone, and especially with her, to prove he was still alive. Maybe that was why he hadn't spoken to her. They'd had enough bad timing already.

He stopped at an intersection just in time to see a car bust the light northbound. He watched it go. The driver, a single Hispanic female in a two-year-old compact, didn't even notice him in the marked police vehicle. Kopriva saw no other cars in the area. He let the car go, turning southbound and continuing his patrol.

***

"Was that him?" Morris asked as they passed a police car.

"No," T-Dog answered. "That was some bitch."

"Are you sure?"

T-Dog nodded.

"Man, you are a no-finding motherfucker, you know that?" Morris took a slug from his forty-ouncer. "Couldn't find your dick to piss with it," he muttered.

T-Dog ignored him. Morris would treat him differently after they found the cop. And after he came back from Compton, beat in and proud.

***

It was a slow Tuesday night. Units made stops all night long and most cleared One-David (No citation issued). Calls for service were few and tapered off around two in the morning. At four-thirty, units began to request sevens. Radio had no reason to refuse and by four-forty-five, the first unit had checked out at Mary's Café for breakfast. Most of the Adam Sector cars quickly followed and after a short time, most of Baker, too.

That left three cars in each sector still on patrol. Down in the radio room, Janice Koslowski felt no alarm at the thinness of patrol. She could have run the whole north side with two cars tonight, much less the six that were still out there. As long as at least one car stayed in service on each side of Division, she didn't see a problem.

***

Thomas Chisolm heard the sevens begin and decided to stay in the field and shag calls. He'd stopped at some Mexican drive-through around midnight and eaten slowly while sitting up at Haven and Illinois, gazing out over the Looking Glass River and the southern half of the city. Now the burrito sat in his stomach like lead shot.

He'd heard yesterday that Payne was reviewed by

the FTO Board at Bates's recommendation and fired. He hadn't been lucky enough to see Hart since the announcement, but he didn't care. The arrogant prick had been wrong and now he had to know it. He wondered briefly if he could force Hart to reinstate him into the FTO program and knew he would probably not have to.

Simply asking nicely would be enough.

Chisolm smiled and turned up the stereo as the Rolling Stones came on singing something about satisfaction.

***

Kopriva considered going to Mary's Café, but he didn't like the fact it was in the extreme northwest of town and almost all the city's units were already there. The only other option was the Denny's at Wellesley and Utah. He headed that direction until he heard Katie's voice over the radio.

"Adam-116, I'll be seven and paperwork at Wellesley and Utah."

Kopriva frowned. He wasn't ready to deal with Katie yet, if he ever would be. Not hungry anyway, he decided to stay in service and drive around. He rolled down the window and turned up the stereo, trying to drive the foggy sleepiness out of his eyes. Some coffee would be nice.

***

Chisolm stopped in a dry cleaning parking lot and backed his car right up to the windows. The lot was at the eastern edge of his sector here, but he could respond to any call quickly enough. Especially on a slow morning like this. He remembered the unofficial graveyard motto. "You know it's a good night when you get to drive fast, point your gun at somebody and take them to jail."

Well, he made a warrant arrest on a stop earlier that night, but it had all gone off pretty low-key. So he stood one-for-three. Of course, some officers were one-for-three as they ripped out of the basement sally-port and raced to the Signal Five for gas.

Chisolm removed the folded burglary report from the visor above him. All that remained to do was to write a brief narrative, one he had written almost verbatim hundreds of times before.

Complainant left at 0700 hrs and returned home at 2200 hrs to find the front door forced open. The residence had been ransacked. Refer to property sheet for missing items. Complainant had no suspects. No physical evidence beyond the damage to the point of entry was found. End of report.

Chisolm still felt sorry for these people, even after all these years of taking similar reports. Most were law-abiding folks whose only contact with the police was when he showed up at their burglary, looking concerned but unable to do much. He wished he could do more, but he couldn't.

So he wrote the report.

***

"That's him," T-Dog said.

Morris snapped straight up in his seat, where he'd been reclining glumly. His beer ran out hours ago and the effects of the alcohol had worn off. He'd considered dozing, but didn't trust T-Dog to spot their target. Maybe he'd been wrong about the guy, after all.

He saw the cop roll by slowly in his marked car. Sure enough, that was the motherfucker.

"Follow him. And not too close."

T-Dog pulled in behind the police car, shadowing it from a block and a half back.

***

Kopriva rubbed his scratchy eyes. The far southeast part of his sector was usually full of activity, but not tonight. Hardly any cars moved and the airwaves were dead. He pulled down Market and decided he would get his coffee at the Circle K at Tyler. He needed to stretch his legs.

***

"Remember, bitch, this ain't no drive-by," Morris told T-Dog. "I want to be sure on this motherfucker. So get your white ass out of the car with me and walk up. Got it?"

T-Dog nodded. The police car, now three blocks ahead, signaled and turned into a convenience store parking lot.

Morris reached down for the fifteenth or twentieth time and felt the cool metal of his .380.

"This is it," he said, his voice high-pitched with excitement. "He's stopping."

***

Kopriva shut off his headlights out of habit as he swung into the Circle K at Market and Tyler. As he pulled up to the front of the store, just to the north of the doors, his mind did a double-take.

A short, slender white male with long black hair was holding a gun on the clerk inside.

"Holy Christ," he whispered and reached for his mike. "Baker-123, robbery in progress at Market and Tyler."

***

Janice sat upright in her chair, dropping the novel she'd been reading. She punched the alarm tone broadcast as she adjusted her headset, then cleared her throat before depressing the foot petal to make the city-wide broadcast.

***

James Mace heard the loud, shrill tone burst from the small radio behind the counter.

"What the fuck is that?" he growled at the clerk.

"P-police scanner," the terrified woman stammered.

A stoic female voice came over the radio, *"Dispatch to all units. Armed robbery in progress at Market and Tyler. Further information to follow."*

"You hit the fucking alarm?" Mace yelled, infuriated.

"No, I didn't hit any—"

He raised the gun and fired twice, shooting the woman in the face. He didn't even blink as wet scalp and skull splattered against the wall behind her. He grabbed the money and headed for the door.

***

Linda Anderson had waited tables at Mary's Café for three years. Never before had she seen every cop in the place empty out for a call. Their sudden exodus forced her to slide into a booth to avoid being trampled as they rushed out and caused her to drop the huge tray laden with breakfast food, covering the floor in a mixture of eggs, bacon and French toast.

***

Kopriva stood behind the door of his patrol car, one leg on the pavement and one leg against the doorjamb. He wedged his back squarely against the car frame. That protected the majority of his body with the engine block. The radio mike sat on the driver's seat, within quick reach.

He witnessed the robber shoot the female clerk in the head and had to resist the urge to run inside, knowing she was already dead. Instead, he drew a bead on the robber inside the store and waited patiently. He felt suddenly very grateful that the department had transitioned to the .40-caliber auto-loaders the year before. They were virtual cannons compared to the .38's the police used to carry.

He was so intent on the distant wail of sirens in the cool morning air, that he did not hear the sound of two car doors being opened behind him.

***

Mace burst out through the glass doors of the Circle K and saw the cop and his car.

"Police! Don't move!" boomed the powerful voice.

Mace didn't bother with a reply, answering with two quick shots.

***

"Police! Don't move!" Kopriva's voice sounded thin and squeaky to him. No authority. No wonder the robber's response was to shoot.

Kopriva returned fire without conscious thought, believing he was firing blindly. He barely recognized the mechanics that his body and mind went through routinely as they had been trained.

Focus on the front sight.

Light bars equal.

Center mass on the fuzzy target.

Squeeze the trigger. Don't pull.

In one second, Kopriva snapped off three shots and watched as the bullets threw the robber backward into the outdoor ice cooler.

***

Mace slammed into a hard wall and lost his wind. He felt the gun slip from his hand as he slid slowly down to his buttocks. He took two shallow breaths. He heard more shots, but felt nothing.

With an effort, he forced himself to his knees, then erect, leaning on the ice cooler for balance. His right hand on the cooler, then the wall, he forced himself to flee in a staggering, shuffling gait.

Move it, Ranger!

In his left hand, he clutched the paper bag, still full of money.

***

As if in answer to his own three shots, Kopriva heard more shots. But the robber had dropped his gun and was sliding down the ice cooler. Echoes?

Behind! These shots were coming from behind him.

In the same instant, he felt a hot pain enter his upper back and explode out his chest, causing a shattering pain in his left collarbone. Wetness bathed his face as he rocked forward, then pitched violently backwards as a smashing force struck behind his left knee. He hit the pavement with a sickening thud, cracking his head on the hard asphalt. He felt hot air and heard a whizzing sound as pavement was chipped away and showered his face.

The morning is so dark, he thought to himself.

***

Morris and T-Dog emptied their magazines, firing at the cop in tandem. Gun enthusiasts called the method "spray-and-pray" and looked upon it with disdain as the only refuge of the poor marksman. Morris didn't care about that shit, though. All he cared about was what he saw—that bitch cop went down and went down *hard*.

***

T-Dog saw the same thing and felt a sense of exhilaration shoot through his body. He looked at the small, black auto. The slide was locked to the rear and smoke curled slowly out of the now-empty chamber.

They'd done it. Now all they had to do was get away with it.

He gave a victory whoop, turned and trotted back to the car. He was surprised to see Morris walk swiftly toward the fallen cop.

Of course, T-Dog realized. *He wants to be sure.*

***

Morris stood above the cop and looked down. He tried to be smug, but he was too jacked up.

"You aren't such a bad-ass after all, are you, cracker?" He spat in the cop's face and raised his pistol to finish him off.

A head shot, Morris decided, *so the casket would have to be closed.*

***

Kopriva heard words as if he were underwater. Something wet splatted against his face. He forced his eyes open.

Morris stood above him, aiming a pistol at his face. It had to be a .45, the barrel looked so huge.

Kopriva didn't hesitate. He pushed himself to the right using his good leg, turning like a top. Morris fired and the bullet crashed into Kopriva's left arm, just above the elbow.

He lifted his own pistol. It felt heavy. He knew it wavered as he fired. He fired as many times as he could. The gunfire sounded liked tiny pops. He counted five pops before his strength gave out and his gun hand fell to his lap.

Kopriva took shallow wavering breaths and gathered his strength.

He knew the fight wasn't over yet.

***

"Fuck me!" T-Dog watched as the cop blasted away at Morris, huge booming explosions that threw Morris back several yards to the ground, where he lay crumpled and broken.

T-Dog saw the cop lay still and thought for a moment that they were both dead. Then he heard Morris moan in pain. The cop twitched and then struggled onto his right elbow.

"Fuck this!" T-Dog ran to the car, jumped in and floored it, heading south on Market.

***

Kopriva heard the squeal of tires and knew the other shooter was gone. All he'd seen of that suspect was his white skin. He set his gun on his lap and pulled himself into a sitting position, his back against the running board of the open door. He reached for the mike on the driver's seat, watching Morris moan and writhe in pain.

***

Morris had never been shot. A lot of gang bangers had, especially in Compton, and they all said it only hurt for a minute. Morris decided that they were all liars. All his wounds were in the hip and groin area. He knew bones had been shattered. It hurt so bad that he couldn't sit still, but every movement only caused him to scream out in pain.

Morris wondered if he were dying.

He saw the .380 lying several feet in front of him. He began to crawl painfully toward it, away from the officer.

If I'm gonna die, that motherfucker is going with me.

***

"Goddamn this bucket of bolts!" Chisolm cursed, flooring the patrol car. With eighty-seven thousand miles on the engine, it had little power. Chisolm asked for everything it had, which wasn't much. He felt the wheels slip in the corners and the transmission clunk as he shifted manually to get the best speed he could.

"Come on," he urged. He was still at least a minute away.

***

Kopriva keyed the mike. "Baker-123. Signal-99. Shots fired. I'm hit."

He dropped the mike back onto the driver's seat, his head swimming.

***

Janice felt her lip tremble as she repeated the signal-99. "All units respond, Tyler and Market. Shots fired, officer down. Channel is restricted for Baker-123 only. All other units use data channel." She motioned to another dispatcher, who plugged into the data channel and began sending units.

"I need medics at Tyler and Market, now!" she called out to her supervisor, Carrie Anne, who was already on the phone.

Hold on, Kopriva, she thought to herself, then keyed her mike.

***

Morris reached the gun, clutching it hard in his right hand. The slide wasn't locked to the rear. He had at least one shot left.

He could feel both his legs all the way to his toes. At least he wasn't crippled.

Morris rolled over and took aim.

***

Kopriva fired one-handed, the gun barking in his strong hand. He saw a spray of blood in Morris' right forearm and knew he'd hit his target. The gun in Morris' hand flew backward as Morris rolled over once and ended up facing him again.

Kopriva lowered his gun. The stabbing pain had subsided to a dull throb. He mused that everyone had been right, after all. This is what he got for being such a code-four cowboy.

"Baker-123, your status?"

He placed the gun in his lap and reached for the mike again. "Two suspects down. One fled. White male. Brown Chevy." He took several shallow breaths while Janice re-broadcast the information.

"Who is it?" he croaked at Morris.

"Fuck you," groaned Morris.

Kopriva swallowed and noted the coppery taste of blood. "Hear those sirens? Nobody here but me and you till they get here." He placed the mike on the driver's seat again.

"Fuck you," Morris repeated. It came out as a low moan.

Kopriva lifted his pistol from his lap, steadied his

aim and fired. He watched with satisfaction and the bullet exploded through Morris's calf. A shrill screech escaped the gang banger's lips.

"You want to be alive when the ambulance comes?" Kopriva asked in between breaths. "Who's the other guy?"

Morris moaned weakly.

Kopriva raised his pistol again, feeling very weak.

"T-Dog," Morris told him.

***

"Baker-123. White male. Moniker T-Dog."

"Copy," Janice said, typing furiously.

"Medics en route," Carrie Anne called.

"Copy," Janice said, noting the time in the computer.

She slid over one terminal and ran the nickname T-Dog with a white male. The computer accepted the entry. It seemed to take an eternity searching through the database, flashing the message "Checking" over and over again.

She got a hit. She did a display entry and read quickly, then keyed the mike with the foot pedal.

***

"Baker-123, I have a white male, Gerald Anthony Trellis. Is that your subject?"

"Trellis?" he tried to shout at Morris, but his voice was getting weaker. Morris surprised him by answering.

"Yeah."

Kopriva keyed the mike. "Affirm."

"Copy. -123, medics are en route. Hold on."

Kopriva clicked his mike and let it fall to the seat.

***

Morris used his left hand to ease the two-shot derringer from his back pocket. He'd only told the cop about T-Dog to buy time. What did he care about that dumb motherfucker, anyway? White bread piece of shit left him to die. What a pussy.

The derringer felt heavy in his hand. He lay across his arm and realized he would have to roll back to free it. He tried to but failed. The pain in his legs was gone, but so was the feeling.

He tried to flop his right arm down in front of him. Maybe he could push himself backward.

***

The sirens were getting closer, Kopriva could tell. He watched Morris for a moment as the gang member seemed to shudder and twitch. He thought about covering him with his gun until back up arrived, but realized he didn't have enough strength left to lift his gun.

His head lolled back, resting against the driver's

seat. He looked up in the sky at the moon. It hung in the early morning darkness, a tinge of yellow cast over it.

We live and work under that moon every night, Kopriva thought, his thoughts becoming disjointed now. *And now I will die here, under a raging moon.*

Kopriva drew a wet, shuddering breath and let it out slowly.

***

Chisolm took the corner hard "Hold on!" he whispered, knowing that Kopriva couldn't hear him. The rear end of the car swung out from under him. He punched the accelerator and the tires struggled for a grip on the pavement, then lurched forward.

***

Morris lay motionless. He'd tried three times to get his left arm out from underneath him, all without success. Impotently, his left fist clutched the derringer, while his right arm hung useless, his fingers resting on the pavement. He felt the wet warmth of his own blood there.

With great effort, he looked up and saw the cop wasn't moving.

Good. Maybe the motherfucker was already dead.

The sirens were very close now, and Morris found that he was glad to hear them.

***

Chisolm slammed on the brakes and put the car into park. He made it out of the car before it even stopped rocking. Pistol out, he approached the scene. He saw the downed suspect lying motionless, eyes closed. As he drew near the police car, he spotted Kopriva seated on the pavement, leaning back into the open driver's doorway. The officer's gun lay in his lap. Chisolm noticed empty casings on the pavement near him.

Chisolm trained his gun on the downed suspect and moved forward quickly. Once close enough, he rolled the suspect forward onto his stomach and put his knee across his neck.

Then he saw the derringer in the suspect's left hand.

The hand twitched.

Chisolm's free hand shot down, grasping the suspect's wrist. A low moan escaped the injured man's lips. Chisolm holstered his pistol and removed the derringer from the suspect's grip. There was no resistance. Either the man was too weak to put up a fight or he simply surrendered. Chisolm quickly cuffed the wounded man behind the back and made his way to Kopriva.

He set the derringer on the ground next to Kopriva. He pulled the uniform shirt back and examined the officer's wounds. One through the upper back. Looked like it entered where the vest panel was thin and exited at the collarbone. The bone stuck out of the wound, a compound fracture.

"Try not to move," Chisolm told Kopriva softly.

He continued to check for wounds. Another one in the left arm, just above the elbow. Blood coursed from that wound.. There was a third injury in his left knee, a huge hole in the kneecap. Painful, but not life-threatening.

Chisolm rose and ran back to the handcuffed suspect. Rolling him over, he searched until he found what he wanted. Hanging from his right front pocket was a blue bandanna. Blue, the color for all Crips. Chisolm took it without a hint of irony.

Kopriva's eyelids fluttered and he groaned when Chisolm wrapped the bandanna tightly around the wound in his upper arm. The pain had probably roused him.

"Tom?" he whispered weakly.

"Yeah, Stef, it's me. Hold tight. You're gonna be fine." He forced a smile. "You're just lucky that bangers are such terrible shots."

The corners of Kopriva's mouth twitched, as if he were trying to return the grin.

"Scarface," he whispered, coughing blood. He pointed toward the store.

Chisolm looked up and saw matted slide marks smeared on the ice-cooler by the door to the convenience store. A small revolver lay on the pavement. A moment later, he saw the trail of blood that lead to the corner of the store, where the light ended. He looked back to Kopriva.

"Scarface." Kopriva mouthed the word more than

said it. With his right hand he held up four fingers. Code four. "Go."

Chisolm considered for a moment. Kopriva was badly hurt, but he knew of nothing more he could do for him. The suspect lay handcuffed and barely conscious himself. But what if Kopriva died? He couldn't let the man die alone.

Chisolm hesitated. In all his experience, he'd learned that most men could sense when they were going to die. Without exception, they did not wish to die alone. It was a true test that he had used on more than one occasion. Especially if the man had stones. Kopriva was a tough kid. If he wasn't asking Chisolm to stay, he probably wasn't going to die.

Chisolm grabbed Kopriva's four fingers and squeezed. "Medics are on the way, cowboy. You'll be fine?"

Kopriva nodded.

Chisolm nodded back and set off in the direction of the blood trail.

***

Kopriva felt his confidence fade as soon as Chisolm left his sight.

He'd often morbidly wondered what, or who, he would be thinking about as he lay dying. He found his mind strangely empy.

He blinked slowly and stared at the moon that raged above.

***

Matt Westboard used Illinois, a wide road that ran diagonally from Perry to Market. He hit one-hundred and ten miles per hour before he had to slow for the upcoming curve onto Market.

Then he saw a white four-door Chrysler at Haven and Grace, one very short block to the north. He locked up his tires. A small, single driver.

Westboard whipped through the empty restaurant parking lot, lighting up the car from the front. A single, white female sat in the passenger seat, her eyes wide with surprise and terror. He noticed that the driver's rear window was rolled down, though the front window was up.

Westboard gave his location channel two and requested a thirteen as soon as Kopriva's scene was secure. He exited his patrol car smoothly and took a knee at his vehicle's front tire. In one fluid motion, he rested his elbows on the hood of his car and pointed his gun directly at the woman, a skinny version of the woman in the photo from the driver's license that had been found lying next to Karl Winter.

Westboard put his laser sight right on her forehead. He decided he would give her one warning, which was more than Karl got.

"Do not move," he yelled over the sound of his rotators. "Keep your hands on the steering wheel or I will blow your head off."

**

The small field to the south of the Circle K should have been an easy escape route for James Mace.

About three short blocks and he could hop into the trunk through the rigged back seat of the car.

But it wasn't as easy as that when you've been shot.

He'd staggered a few feet after letting go of the store wall. Then he had fallen.

Never quit, he had told himself.

Once a Ranger, always a Ranger.

He crawled, pulling with his arms, pushing with his legs. The paper bag tore and he knew some of the money was falling from his grasp, but enough remained. Enough to get some underground medical attention and still get a fix.

He moved another two feet, paused, breathing. He hoped Carla kept her cool and waited.

The sirens were very close, all around now.

Never quit, he muttered soundlessly and continued to crawl.

***

Chisolm rounded the corner, gun in hand. He saw no running figures and no trees to hide behind.

He followed the blood smears down the wall several yards, where they ended. He turned and spotted a police car in the distance, rotating blue and red lights and a flood of white.

Did they have him up there?

Chisolm took several steps, then saw the drag marks in the grass. He hesitated, remembering 'Nam and the ambush at Bai-trang in the Mekong Delta. He'd followed those drag marks for over a mile before finding the wounded sniper. He hadn't seen any need for interrogation, not after having watched Bobby Ramirez's head explode right next to him and shower him with his best friend's blood. With a crazed smile on his face, he'd pumped all eight rounds from his .45 into that VC's head.

The drag marks went due south.

Chisolm followed them as he squeezed the gun in his hand.

***

Katie MacLeod screeched to a stop and exited her car, weapon drawn. She surveyed the scene and saw the handcuffed suspect.

Then she saw Kopriva, still and unmoving.

***

James Mace knew he was going to make it now. His bleeding had slowed, almost stopped, and he felt strong enough to make it to the car.

Go, Ranger! Never quit!

He kept crawling.

***

The grass, swaying with the early morning breeze,

still showed traces of blood as Chisolm tracked the injured man. The blood appeared black in pre-dawn light combined with distant street lights, but flared red when his flashlight illuminated the thin streaks in the grass. He could tell by the drag marks that the suspect was not frantic yet, that he kept a cool head. Chisolm pointed his weapon ahead of himself, always at the threat.

He passed a black wig and kept walking.

Stray, crumpled bills marked the trail. He followed, his jaw set.

Twenty yards from the edge of the field, over two blocks from the store, Chisolm spotted him. He moved slowly now, but steadily, always forward. He clutched a wad of bills tightly in his left hand. The right hand was empty, grasping at the ground in front of him and pulling.

Unarmed.

Maybe.

Chisolm thought for a moment.

Probably. He'd seen the gun back at the store.

Chisolm holstered his pistol and slid his flashlight into its holder. The blood streaks were smaller now, almost nonexistent in the suspect's trail. The bleeding had almost stopped and Scarface was still moving... which meant he would probably live.

Which meant he would stand trial. And possibly be acquitted.

This sonofabitch gunned down Winter! Chisolm felt a surge of rage. He reached for his pistol, but stopped. He couldn't shoot an unarmed man. All the wounds the robber had were from Kopriva's gun. There would be no justification for Chisolm to shoot.

Gun dropped back at the scene...

Chisolm made his decision in an instant. He moved as soundlessly as possible up behind the suspect and fell upon him.

***

Katie took Kopriva's hand and squeezed it as hard as she could. "Stef?"

She thought for sure he was dead until he groaned and weakly opened his eyes.

"Stef? It's all right. I'm here. It's Katie." Tears welled up in her eyes. "I'm here."

***

Chisolm drove his knee downward toward the nape of the suspect's neck. He was rewarded with a sickening snap. The man went motionless.

Chisolm grabbed a handful of hair and rotated the man's neck. The floppy, circular motion told him all he needed to know. He took a deep breath and yelled, "Police! Don't move! Don't resist!"

Forcing the suspect's limp hands behind his back, Chisolm keyed his mike.

"Adam-112, I've got a suspect at the south edge of the field—" he let the mike button up and counted two seconds. "He's resisting." He let the button up again and cuffed the dead suspect with his second pair of cuffs.

His report would read that the suspect had resisted arrest as he attempted prone-cuffing. Everyone in the department knew that prone-cuffing was the proper procedure to use with a dangerous felon. Sometimes the felon was injured.

He keyed the mike, forcing himself to breathe heavily as he spoke. "Adam-112, one in custody. I'll need medics here, too. Injured suspect."

Radio copied his transmission. Chisolm looked down at the motionless suspect.

Sometimes the felon even died.

Chisolm thought about Bobby Ramirez and he thought about Karl Winter and he resisted the urge to kick the unmoving robber until there was nothing recognizable left.

***

Kopriva slowly blinked. He tried to say her name but could only mouth it.

"I'm here, Stef," she told him over and over. "I'm here."

The sound of her voice gave him strength, and he held her hand tightly. Medics arrived and worked on him at a frenetic pace, tearing and cutting clothing, bandaging, applying pressure. Kopriva would not let go of her hand, and she seemed to be doing her best to stay out of the medic's way as she held his grip.

A second ambulance arrived and began to work on Morris. He heard medics ask her to unlock the handcuffs. She handed them her cuff key, refusing to leave Kopriva's side. He stared at her as they slid him onto a backboard, ignoring everything around him. She walked with him to the ambulance and got inside with them. His eyes never left hers, oblivious to the work the medics were doing. He didn't feel the I.V. go in, didn't see anything they did to him.

The ambulance doors slammed shut and he heard two hard taps on the back door. The ambulance lurched forward. The medics did not pause in their efforts.

He continued to stare at her until everything melted into a gray mist and his eyes closed.

Monday, September 2nd
Day Shift

The officer sat in his living room, staring at the television but not seeing it. The service pistol in his right hand felt heavy, but his grip on it was firm.

Several art books adorned his coffee table. He wondered fleetingly if any of his co-workers knew about his knowledge when it came to the subject of art. Probably not. Everyone thought they knew exactly who and what he was, when in reality they had no idea at all.

Just as she had no idea.

He found it oddly humorous that he sat alone in his living room holding a gun, and it was a woman who had eventually put him here.

"Who the fuck cares?" he grumbled, staring at the white ceiling above him. He thought of Da Vinci, of Giotto, of Botticelli. He thought of Michelangelo. He wondered how they would have felt about modern art.

Well, he would create a masterpiece for them to ponder.

He put the gun under his chin, closed his eyes and painted the ceiling red.

***

Lt. Robert Saylor rubbed his eyes, trying to remember the last time he'd slept. Well, after he prepared the press release, he could go home and get a few hours of sleep before he had to come back for the night shift.

What a night. At least Kopriva would make it. The doctors said that Chisolm's light tourniquet probably kept him from bleeding out.

Chisolm. He saved Kopriva and managed to catch Scarface, now identified as James R. Mace. Kopriva's shots hit him twice in the belly, but Mace still crawled away. According to Chisolm's report, Mace had struggled when Chisolm tried to cuff him. He told Saylor with a straight face that he'd been unaware that the man's neck was broken until medics had told him.

Saylor decided that Chisolm was telling the truth. Even if he wasn't.

Matt Westboard caught the accomplice only a block and a half from where Chisolm found Scarface. He took her straight to Major Crimes, where she spilled everything. Westboard had confirmed hearing Chisolm's commands and the struggle with Mace, but he hadn't actually seen anything because he'd been covering the accomplice.

Units were scouring the city for T-Dog, Morris' accomplice and an arrest warrant had been issued based on Kopriva's radio traffic. Detective Browning showed the injured officer a photo line-up as soon as the kid woke up. Kopriva identified Trellis, positively.

Later, Saylor informed Kopriva that Morris remained on the operating table and that he may or may not make it. Either way, he would be a cripple. Kopriva hadn't even tried to suppress a smile before he'd gone back to sleep and the doctor ushered Saylor out of the hospital room.

The lieutenant felt bad for Kopriva. Before he even had a chance to recover from his wounds, the newspaper would question his actions in scathing editorials. Worse yet, Internal Affairs had to begin their mandatory investigation. And the questions they asked were never pleasant.

Saylor wrote his press release carefully, only giving away what information he knew he had to release to satisfy the media.

Goddamn piranhas, he groused.

He'd almost finished when the phone rang.

***

Anthony Giovanni and Mark Ridgeway stood at the door of Sgt. David Poole's residence. Technically, because it was a crime scene, one of them should have been in the rear, guarding the back door, but Ridgeway locked the back door from the inside and came around front. Neither man wanted to be left alone while the County detectives investigated the death of a City officer.

Lt. Hart had left moments earlier and both men were appalled at his lack of emotion. He'd behaved the same way on a dozen other suicide scenes. Officious and overbearing, he talked to Gio and Ridgeway as if they were rookies who didn't know how to secure a crime scene. If he'd known that no one was guarding the back door, it would've tipped him right over the edge.

They were glad for his presence, however, when the media arrived in force. He quickly extended the crime scene out to the middle of the residential street. This allowed only one lane of traffic, which the media vehicles could not block. With all the County cars parked on Poole's side of the road, the closest media vehicle set up shop almost a block away.

They were even happier for Hart's presence when Sherrie, Poole's ex-wife, arrived and tried to enter the house. Hart escorted her away from the scene. She'd been distraught, which was understandable, but it had surprised both of them. Everyone knew why she'd divorced Sgt. Poole.

Neither man said anything, but both knew what the other was thinking. Suicide. The policeman's disease.

Both suspected the other had probably sat in his own living room and stared at the black metal sitting on the table in front of him. Sat and stared and thought. Thought of the woman he had lost. How much of himself he had lost. In her and in the job.

Both wondered if the other had tasted the cool metal that smelled of gunpowder and lubricant. Had his finger slipped into the trigger guard? Had it touched the trigger? Had he shut his eyes, silent tears streaming down his face and wondered what waited on the other side? Was it courage or cowardice that made him release the trigger and set the gun back down with a shaking hand?

Both men considered these questions in silence and waited.

County Sheriff's detectives conducted their investigation. The meticulous process began with photos of the exterior of the house, and worked slowly inward to the scene.

Gio and Ridgeway stood by uncomfortably, wondering if he had left a note.

***

Hospital. Kopriva recognized the antiseptic smells and the subdued, bustling sounds. Slowly, he opened his eyes. Light streamed through his window, warm sunshine on his face.

It felt good.

He tilted his head slightly. Katie sat at his bedside. Tired worry lines creased her face, but they washed away when she smiled at him.

He smiled back, realizing then that she still held his hand.

"Hey," he croaked and tried to smile.

"Hey," she whispered, squeezing his hand. "You gave me quite a scare, Stef."

"Scared me, too." His throat went dry. He thought about asking for some water, but wanted to look at her a moment longer.

She met his gaze and smiled with warm eyes.

***

"Blood pressure?" The doctor asked, knowing he

was losing this one. The patient had already endured a surgery earlier in the day, which had been successful enough to keep him from dying immediately. This second surgery was supposed to keep him from dying at all.

The nurse's answer confirmed what he knew. Too much damage. In the kidney and in the liver, shards of metal were everywhere.

He stepped away from the patient, listening to the long moments between beeps on the heart monitor turn into a steady tone. He sighed as he removed his gloves.

"Time?"

"1557," responded a nurse.

"Note it. And turn that monitor off."

The doctor silently cursed guns, bullets and those who manufactured them. He remained silent as he slipped off the bloody latex gloves and threw them away. He didn't know what religion Isaiah Morris adhered to, if any, but he had no wish to profane the moment of the man's exit from this world.

***

"Is that all, then?" Ridgeway asked the detective.

"Yeah, just lock the front door for us and we're done." The detective held several paper bags of evidence taken from inside the house. "Listen, I'm sorry."

"Yeah. Thanks."

The detective left. Ridgeway locked the front door and turned to face Giovanni.

"I have to put the keys on property."

"Okay."

"You want to meet me at Duke's afterwards?"

"Definitely," Gio answered, nodding.

"See you there, then."

***

Katie's lips pressed lightly against Kopriva's temple. He closed his eyes and soaked in the softness and warmth of her lips and the slight scent of vanilla on her skin. When he heard footsteps and the rustle of a curtain, his eyes snapped open.

Katie started in surprise and pulled her head away. Kopriva glanced at her and saw her cheeks flush.

The nurse only smiled.

"That is the best medicine I know of, girl," she told them. "Love, love, love."

Monday, September 2nd
End of Tour

Johnny poured three quick shots and lifted them onto Rachel's tray. The atmosphere at Duke's was familiar, but he noticed a strange buzz in the crowd. By now, Johnny had heard about Poole and he imagined the sergeant's death had something to do with the way patrons were acting. Some of the regulars knew, too, and they sat and conversed quietly, leaving the cops alone as they entered.

Chisolm had come first, taking a spot at the end of the bar. Johnny knew his drink and brought it without being asked. He noticed that Chisolm seemed neither depressed nor jovial and wondered if the man ever reached the depths of either emotion.

Ridgeway and Giovanni came in next and forewent their usual table to join Chisolm at the bar. Johnny served them as well, again asking no questions. In contrast to Chisolm, both men seemed solemn.

When Katie MacLeod, Matt Westboard and Will Reiser arrived, the group moved to the large table in the corner. Johnny kept Rachel busy bringing them drinks and wished he hadn't sent the new girl home for the day.

"Johnny!" Ridgeway's barked from across the room, his voice slightly slurred. "I want you to meet the man who captured the notorious Scarface Robber." He paused a moment, then continued. "Wait a minute. You didn't catch him, did you, Tom? You killed him. Sorry." The group laughed.

Ridgeway turned back to the bartender. "Never mind, Johnny."

Johnny was used to the gallows humor. He smiled and waved from behind the bar.

Chisolm shook his head. "You're just jealous," he told Ridgeway, setting ı p his favorite joke.

"Why?" Ridgeway played into the old line, even though he'd heard it dozens of times. "Because I don't have to write a fifteen-page report and get grilled by IA?"

"No. You're jealous because I get to eat your wife but not her cooking."

The group broke up in laughter and ooohs. Other patrons listened now and laughed at Chisolm's line.

"You ate my wife?" Ridgeway asked in mock anger.

Chisolm winked and took a sip of his beer.

"Really?" Ridgeway asked. "How'd I taste?"

Everyone laughed even louder, and Chisolm laughed with them, conceding. He could not top that.

***

The doctor stood at Kopriva's bedside. "You will have some loss of strength and range of motion, as I've explained. Particularly in your left arm. You might reach sixty to sixty-five percent mobility with therapy."

"What about the knee?"

"Thanks to sports medicine, we can do a lot to repair knees." The doctor glanced at his clipboard. "You won't be running the Boston Marathon or Bloomsday, but you'll walk, albeit with a limp."

"Will I be able to return to duty?"

"As a patrol officer?" The doctor pressed his lips together and considered. "I can't say for sure. I'd have to see how you respond to treatment and therapy. Then I'd need to get a better idea of the exact physical requirements for your position."

"Sounds like a 'no'," Kopriva said.

The doctor shook his head. "Not at all. Let's just wait and see how things work out. All right?"

"How long do I have to stay here?" Kopriva asked him.

The doctor shrugged. "Another week. Maybe two. I want you completely stabilized and make sure there's no infection before we let you go home. We'll know more in a few days."

Kopriva nodded and the doctor left.

He took a deep breath and let it out, already anticipating the storm that waited for him after he healed. The Monday-morning quarterbacks would pad up and dissect his every move. They'd wanted to do so with Winter, but had kept it to themselves out of respect for the dead. Kopriva lived, so he would be fair game.

He took another deep breath and exhaled. He'd deal with that when it happened. For now, he found himself looking forward to Katie's visit later that afternoon.

***

Everyone was hammered, Johnny knew. He also knew better than to cut anyone off. He would call the taxis when the time came.

"Is Hart working?" Ridgeway asked. "The little pecker."

"Let's find out," Chisolm said, walking to the pay phone. Everyone watched as he put a quarter in and dialed. A few moments later, he spoke.

"Lieutenant Hart, please." There was a pause. Chisolm covered the receiver and said, "They're getting him."

The bar fell completely silent. Then Chisolm spoke into the phone. "Is this Lieutenant Alan Hart? Yes?" Chisolm glanced at the watching crowd and winked. "Well, then fuck you, you pencil-necked prick." He hung up the phone.

The silence turned to disbelief, then exploded into laughter. Chisolm returned to the table, grinning drunkenly.

"What if he recognized your voice?" Westboard asked above the laughter.

"What if he has it analyzed?" Chisolm asked him, sitting down. "Who cares?"

Ridgeway stood, his glass held high. "To Thomas Chisolm, biggest stones in the whole department!"

A roar of laughter followed and everyone drank. Johnny watched as all the patrons in the small bar turned toward the table in the corner. Ridgeway sat down.

"To Stef Kopriva," Katie toasted, "and a speedy recovery."

"Hear, hear," called the group and civilian patrons alike. Everyone drank again.

An uncomfortable silence settled in. Thomas Chisolm rose and stood solemnly, his face regal and hard. The thin white scar he received in Vietnam had never faded and in the small, dark bar, it seemed to glow.

He raised his beer bottle. "To our honored dead," he said. "To Sgt. David Poole."

"Poole," repeated several.

"To Karl Winter," Chisolm bellowed in a hard voice.

The roar rose in unison.

"To Karl Winter."

Epilogue
Fall 1994

The doctor looked at his watch. Fifty minutes had passed since the officer had sat down and now the session had come to an end.

The officer noticed him looking and said, "Our time is up, huh, doc?"

The doctor nodded.

"So what's the verdict?" the officer asked him.

Instead of answering, he asked, "Why don't you tell me?"

"You mean, am I crazy? Whacked out over this shooting?" He shook his head. "No. I'm okay with it. And I'll get through whatever the department is sending my way, too. One way or another."

"Why is that?"

"Because I don't do this job for them," the officer stated simply.

"Why do you do this job then?"

"Aren't we out of time?"

The doctor waved his comment away. "It's fine. We have a few minutes left."

The officer shrugged, then continued. "I do this job to do the right thing. To be on the right side." He paused for a long moment. The doctor was about to ask him another question when he said quietly, "I do this job to make a difference."

The doctor nodded at the common sentiment among police officers. "Have you?" he asked the officer. "Have you made a difference?"

The officer turned to face him, his expression calm.

"Time will tell," he said.

Take a moment to read Chapter One from the next exciting book in the River City series by Frank Zafiro,

Heroes Often Fail

It was a secret place and like most secret places, it was forbidden and dangerous.

Kendra discovered it when she took the long way home from school one day, and immediately shared it with Amy. The two girls swore each other to secrecy in hushed tones, their pinkie fingers locked. Amy was the one who named it the Fairy Castle.

She and Amy didn't want Kendra's brothers or other neighborhood boys finding out about Fairy Castle, so they kept their secret as best they could.

Of course, Amy told her mother everything and so it was only a matter of time before Mrs. Dugger was down at Fairy Castle to check things out.

"Ugh," she'd said. "Girls, this place is so *dirty*."

"You have to use your imagination, Mom," Amy had told her. She swept her hand across the small dirt cave. "This is the ballroom, where we have our dances, and—"

"Amy, honey, this is a cave dug into the side of a pile of dirt and held up by a couple of boards." She pointed to the two pieces of lumber jammed up into the low roof ceiling. "You don't know if animals come in here or other kids—"

"Mom, it's a secret place," Amy told her. "No one knows but us."

Mrs. Dugger shook her head. "It's not safe. I don't want you playing here any more. Do you understand?"

"But, Mom—"

"No buts. You are not allowed to play here any more and that is final."

After Amy's Mom said they couldn't go there any more, Kendra didn't dare tell her parents about Fairy Castle. School was out for a whole week and she and Amy were planning on spending as much time as possible at their secret, forbidden place.

Last night's rain covered the city streets and left behind small puddles in the cracks and holes in the roadway. Kendra jumped in the air and landed in a small puddle, sending a spray of water in Amy's direction.

"Knock it off, Kenny," Amy said, knowing her friend hated being called that.

Kendra frowned for a moment and considered splashing Amy again. She decided not to and quickly caught up to her, skipping her way to Amy's side.

"I think we should have a wedding today," Amy said.

Kendra smiled. A wedding. That was perfect.

"You can be the bride," Amy said, pushing a lock of her dark her behind her ear. Kendra has seen Mrs. Dugger do that, too. "And I'll be your maid of honor."

"What's that?"

"It's like the bride's best friend. She gets to stand next to her while she gets married."

Kendra beamed. She would get to be the bride and have her best friend next to her. What could be better?

"Who will you marry?" Amy asked her.

That was a serious question and Kendra gave it considerable thought.

"And no one from school," Amy blurted. "You have to marry a movie star or some famous person."

Her first inclination was to choose Prince Charming from the movie *Sleeping Beauty*, but he was only a cartoon. She knew Amy would be quick to point that out and then she would just have to choose again, anyway, so she dropped the whole idea and gave it some more deep thought.

The girls turned onto Stevens and headed for the empty lot on the corner, less than half a block from Fairy Castle now. Kendra felt a small surge of panic. She had to decide who she wanted to marry before they reached the secret place. But who?

"I know who I'd marry," Amy whispered.

The sound of a vehicle turning the corner behind them caused both to move to the sidewalk.

"Who?"

Amy gave her a secretive smile. "You can't tell anyone."

Kendra raised her hand, small finger extended. "Pinkie swear."

Amy reached out and locked fingers. "I'd marry Westley."

"Westley who?" she asked

"You know," Amy said, and Kendra did. Westley was a character from their favorite movie, *The Princess Bride*. He was handsome and nice and more importantly, he was real and not a cartoon. Kendra wished she had thought of that first. Maybe—

"That's who I was going to say," she told Amy.

"Too late," Amy teased. "He's going to be my husband and we're getting married tomorrow at Fairy Castle."

"But I'm getting married today."

Amy shrugged. "You'll just have to marry someone else, I guess."

"But I wanted to marry Westley, too."

"Why didn't you say so?"

Kendra bit her lip. "I was…thinking about how my dress should look, that's all."

"Liar," Amy said, shaking her head.

"It's true!"

"Nuh-uh, Kenny."

"I'm not lying—"

There came a chirp of tires coming to a sudden stop and both girls turned their heads to the street. A blue van had pulled to a stop next to them. The side door slid open and a tall, thin man stepped out with a black ski mask over his face.

Kendra's eyes widened and struggled to think of what she was taught to do in these situations.

The man reached for Amy, who stood frozen in place just like her.

She watched the man's white hands grasp Amy by the upper arms and pull her to his chest.

The man's eyes flashed to her and she saw something in them she knew instinctively was bad for her. She sprinted away as fast as her legs would carry her.

The sound of the van door slamming shut and the engine gunning spurred her to run even faster. She knew she couldn't outrun the van and hoped wildly someone would save her before the van screeched to a stop next to her and the man in black gobbled her into his arms, too.

Kendra's heart pounded in her chest, her neck, her temples. She couldn't get enough air into her tiny lungs. But her legs pumped like two pistons, running straight and hard.

The roar of the engine faded and then she found herself alone, too scared even to cry.

Printed in the United States
92461LV00001B/37-45/A